FINAL NIGHT

FINAL NIGHT

THE REVENANT RECORDS
BOOK 1

KELL SHAW

ISBN Ebook: 978-1-922897-00-8

ISBN Audiobook: 978-1-922897-01-5

ISBN Paperback: 978-1-922897-02-2

ISBN Hardback: 978-1-922897-06-0

For Michael

FINAL NIGHT

KELL SHAW

THE REVENANT RECORDS: BOOK ONE

CONTENTS

CHAPTER 1
BEFORE

"DAD!"

The darkness pressed in close. Like a living thing, it wanted to devour her whole.

He came, as she knew he would. Her bedroom door opened, the light clicked on and transformed the abyss into a safe, familiar space. Pink walls. Stuffed unicorns on her chair. Towers of cassettes threatening to topple off the desk.

"Greenie went dark!" Lukie pointed. "And the monsters were coming for me!"

Dad scooped her up in a big hug. His beard scratched her face, and she inhaled his habitual tobacco smell. "Let's fix this."

She hovered near while he inspected the glass unicorn nightlight. "Bulb's gone," he said. "I've got spares." He held her by the hand and took her down the carpeted corridor to the kitchen, where he rummaged in a bottom drawer, sorting past paper bags, rolls of string, and masking tape. "The important thing is no monsters are left. Remember why?"

"Reladon." She clutched the sleeve of his plaid pajamas.

"That's right." Dad pulled out a lightbulb and slipped off the packaging. Holding her hand, he guided her back to her bedroom. "Once upon a time, there was a terrible age of magic and monsters. Dragons burned cities, zombies dragged people from their houses, and krakens swallowed up entire ships. That was when the Dark Emperor ruled, enslaving the world with his nightmare legions. But then all the brave heroes got together, formed the Alliance of Light, and fought the Dark Emperor at the Battle of Reladon. And who saved everyone?"

He pushed the bedroom door open, and Lukie bit her fingers nervously while he screwed the new bulb inside of Greenie.

"Hawkbow!"

"General Hawkbow," Dad agreed. "She had an enchanted arrow created by the last wizards of the Crystalspire. Her aim was true, and she shot the Dark Emperor right through his heart. And when she did, one of the moons, Marmaruk, shattered into a ring that encircled the entire world, and the Age of Magic ended."

Dad snapped his fingers. "No more monsters. All the horrible things—ghosts, faeries, demons, and dragons—were sealed away forever. All the races who stayed in the mortal world—elves, dwarrow, and ogres—lost their powers and everyone became ordinary people. We made friends with each other as there was no need to fight each other since the Dark Emperor was gone." He snapped his fingers again. "And no more magic. The wizards had to get jobs at the shops and libraries. And, after a while, no one missed their wands and spells, as we invented technology instead. Like your nightlight."

With a dramatic flourish, he clicked it on, spilling warm, buttery light.

"You saved her!"

"Technology is amazing." Dad smiled. "In the old days, we'd have to get a wizard in, and he'd cost a fortune. Now, back to bed." He held up her covers, and Lukie crawled under pink layers of sheets and blankets.

"I want Mama."

Dad stroked her hair. "Sweetie, remember she's in the Precursor's Garden. Waiting. You'll see her someday, but not yet." He took a deep breath. "I know it's bad your mother isn't here. It's a big change. Think of how the people must have felt when they lost all the magic. But the world was still there, only different, and full of wonderful new things to discover and explore. One day, when you're a lot older and have had so many adventures, we'll be with Mama again. And you'll have heaps of stories to tell her."

She reached out for her bedside table, for the framed photograph of when they'd all been together for their last Winterdark Festival. She clutched it tight to her chest like a promise as Dad kissed her and left the room, the nightlight glowing in the corner.

She was safe. She repeated all the things Dad told her. No magic. No monsters. She'd see Mama again one day. And everything would be all right.

But he had lied.

CHAPTER 2
AWAKENING

7:53PM, 7 BLOODSTONE 1983 (?)

SHE HAD no idea how she got here.

Sand. A lapping tide. Confused, Lukie struggled to her feet. Water sloshed in her boots, and she was cold all over like she'd been at her after-school job stacking the freezer section at Cubermarket.

The ocean was dark and heaving, the sky above colored in bands of lavender and gold. Far to the south she glimpsed the shadowy edges of the Pillars of Majesty—limestone formations spearing out of the sea along the coastal King's Road. A late summer sunset. Later than… when?

You'll have until dawn… Her memories were jumbled. *Running from hungry shadows. Hiding in the darkness. An impassioned conversation. Crawling out and upward through a pipe for a long time.*

Which didn't explain anything. She looked around, then down, and clawed wet sand off her jacket.

Light glinted off Marmaruk, the thin planetary ring that girdled the overhead sky. His sister, Amarun—the surviving moon—rose above him, her face a slender crescent.

Wait, hadn't the moon been full earlier? Lukie scratched grit from her hair. She faced the steep cliff. On the top was the old beach house where the party had been.

Oh yeah. She'd been there. She remembered…

Well, nothing clearly. Spook Club. Holding her guitar. The music. A blur of voices and faces. But not how she had gotten to the beach.

She recalled a dark tunnel. Stairs leading upwards with worn carpet. A voice: *You'll have until dawn…*

To do *what?*

It had to be the *same* evening. She must have been confused about the moon. Time to get back to the party and find out what was going on.

If this was a sick joke, she'd punch the people responsible. Repeatedly.

Lukie patted herself down.

She was wearing familiar clothes. Amber bangles. Outside Sky t-shirt. Red leather jacket. In one pocket were the keys to her new—okay, *newish*—car. In the other was a cassette, a home recording of her own composition that had helped her gain admission into Storm City's Conservatorium of Music. And in the other, a photograph of her family taken when they'd been on their last holiday together at Storm City for Winterdark. Before Mom had passed.

I never brought these with me. The keys, yes. But the cassette and their final family photo had been tucked in her special drawer in her bedroom. They weren't wet; her jacket had kept them dry.

Am I dreaming? She poked herself. She felt that. But her skin was nearly frozen. *I need to get somewhere warm before I die of hypothermia.*

Lukie staggered toward the cliff.

Something else was wrong. The stairs were in the right position, but now with a wooden railing. Maybe Nathel's parents had installed it before the party. *Wouldn't I have remembered it, though?* She hurried upward to the beach house.

And things got strange.

The structure *should* have been there. All gleaming glass and steel. Drunken people sitting under the porch. The boom of music from inside, the clink of glasses, and the smell of beer. She even expected cruel laughter as she clambered up the steps, wet and thoroughly pissed off, clearly the victim of a practical joke.

Instead, there was just a lonely, weed-infested ruin. Peeling paint covered the stucco walls. The window frames were empty, revealing a scarred concrete slab and an interior dusted with sand.

This wasn't right.

She ran past the abandoned place, down the overgrown driveway. If this had been the actual site of the house, her car would have been parked *there*. But it wasn't.

Now what? Perhaps she was at the incorrect location. Or she was on a macabre prank TV show.

But the area was too real, too familiar to be elsewhere. And there was no camera in sight.

Every time things went wrong in life, she saw Dad. He sorted out her worst problems, made it all right again.

So she ran home to Breakwater Bay.

Lukie had spent her entire life in the small town. It was one of many that dotted the east coast, popular with tourists who came to surf on the golden beaches during summer or to visit the region's historical mansions during the winter. It should have taken her an hour to hike into town, but it felt like only minutes had passed when she arrived.

But as Lukie reached the outskirts, a sense of wrongness slammed into her senses like an unhealed wound.

As she remembered things, Endeavor Drive, the central street, ran directly in front of the beach, lined with ocean-facing brown brick cottages and fibro houses. A large wharf speared down the main beach, and around it clustered bars, fast-food restaurants, and bait and tackle shops.

But as she followed the street, her attention was snagged by a giant shopping mall and bowling alley that hadn't been there earlier this evening. Strange cars drove past; only a few recognizable models, and all of those were battered and worn. Small high-rise apartment blocks clustered along the beachfront streets rather than the familiar homes.

She zigzagged back and forth across the road, staring at the street signs. Bream Road. Seaview Plaza. Catch Lane. Surfside Drive—that wasn't right! Why—

A car crunched into her.

She slammed against the hood and bounced against the blacktop like a ragdoll.

Brakes squealed. A woman screamed from inside the vehicle.

Lukie sprawled on her back.

Her left arm was bent wrong.

Bone was sticking out of it like a snapped twig.

But it didn't hurt. Sure, it itched. But there was no pain. And no blood.

Am I on drugs? She clenched her teeth as black, oozing smoke trickled out of the cuts in her skin. Under the shadowy mass, gray tendons knitted together.

So freaky!

Oily black vapor briefly encircled the protruding bone. It faded away, leaving a healed wound and unmarked pallid flesh. *What is this dark stuff? It feels almost sentient. It leaked out of me—*

"Are you alright?" A huge man loomed over her. "I'm so sorry! We were talking, and I wasn't watching the road."

Lukie blinked, staring at the car that had hit her. It was

sleek, with red chrome stylings, and like no design she'd ever seen.

There were four people around her—university-age twenty-somethings dressed strangely in low-rise jeans without flared ends, sparkly lip gloss, and flat, straightened hair. The big man had obvious ogre ancestry. There was a curly-haired human woman and two dwarrow, which was weird because in Lukie's experience, different hominins rarely mingled with each other.

"I'm checking you for broken bones!" The woman patted Lukie down. "She's like ice. Get me the picnic blanket." When she touched Lukie, a smooth brassy dance beat thumped in the air.

"I'm fine!" Lukie got to her feet and pushed the woman away.

The music cut out. And *that* didn't make any sense either.

But Lukie was more distracted by her own voice than some weird hidden radio. It had come out slow and raspy, like she had a bad cold.

Her left foot straightened, and bones clicked into place. She tested it. *Needs a bit longer.*

"Stay down. You could have a serious injury! We need to call an ambulance."

"Maybe she knows what she's doing, Maz." The big man put his arms around the curly-haired woman. "It might be an elf thing."

"I'm human," Lukie insisted, despite feeling the heat rise in her pointed ears as the others stared with disbelief. But her grandmother's people were insistent: half an elf was *not an elf.* She desperately tried to clear her throat. "And I'm fine." She jumped up and down, demonstrating her fitness. "You braked just in time." Her voice remained husky.

"See, she's okay." The ogre wiped the sweat from his face.

"Are you sure?" One of the dwarrow women put her hands on her hips. "She looks like a zombie to me."

Lukie's stomach churned. *Zombie?* An ice-cold sensation speared through her left leg. She stamped her foot—ready for walking. "Uh, I'm going to a party."

"The one in the hills?" Maz said. "We're heading there. We can give you a lift. Love your 80s costume and your spooky contacts. Perfect for Final Night."

"What's that?" Lukie asked.

Maz and her ogre friend glanced at each other and then back at Lukie.

"You know," Maz spoke slowly. "It's a horror party about those girls who got murdered twenty years ago. It's the only reason people come to the sticks this time of year. Hey, are you sure you don't want a ride to the hospital?"

Murdered?

Twenty years?

No, no. There has to be an explanation for this.

"I have to go!" Lukie fled, despite them calling out to her. Something was wrong with her—and the town—and she needed to figure out what it was. She shoved past a group of onlookers, nearly collided with a confused tourist in a baseball cap eating a burger, and sprinted through the neon-lit streets to the first sign of safety: a public restroom that had been there this morning.

The bathroom was still there. Painted white now, but the same. Five stalls, graffitied doors, dirty cream tiles, stainless steel sink and taps, an empty paper towel dispenser.

Her blurred reflection stared back at her from smeared glass.

Red, luminous eyes. Deathly skin.

She looks like a zombie to me.

Lukie clenched the bathroom sink and inhaled deeply to

steady herself. And then she realized she hadn't been breathing at all.

CHAPTER 3
DEAD REFLECTION

8:17PM, 7 BLOODSTONE 2003

LUKIE FACED the mirror above the sink. Most of her appearance was familiar. Spiked blonde hair, black jeans, chunky amber bangles, and her red leather jacket, of course. Just how she'd dressed for the party.

But her eyes were a luminous crimson, and speckled with tiny dark blots. No iris or pupil. She rubbed them, hoping to find contacts. She squished and dug, but no lenses came off on her fingertips.

Her green eyes were gone. She consciously breathed in and out. The usual public convenience stink flooded her nostrils.

Then she held her breath and waited for her lungs to ache. For tension to flood her body. Nothing happened. At least the toilets had stopped smelling.

Minutes dragged by. She wasn't breathing, and she was still... there. She exhaled with a rattling hiss. When she paid attention, she breathed; was that a habit? A living habit.

But undead? They only exist in books and movies. Not real life.

She clutched the steel sink. All children grew up knowing this was the era of technology. All the magic and monsters in the world had gone away when General Hawkbow killed the

Dark Emperor at the Battle of Reladon two thousand years ago. No one cared anymore apart from nerds. Even her history teacher at school had been skeptical about the so-called 'Age of Magic.' There were no dragon bones in the fossil record, and when scientists had tested the legendary magical sword Joyous Strike, it had displayed no special properties.

She lived in a scientific, rational world. Zombies didn't exist.

I can't be undead! There has to be a medical reason for this. And if I were undead, wouldn't I have to be dead to begin with?

She tore off her jacket, t-shirt, and bra. If she'd died, there would be marks.

And there were.

Her throat was ringed with blood-colored bruises. Red scratches ran down her breasts. More contusions spotted her chest and stomach. She gingerly poked at them, especially the ones around her neck, but they didn't feel sore, only colder to the touch than the rest of her skin.

Someone had strangled her.

"I'm not dead," she shouted—if she was alive, her throat would have hurt—and hit the sink. The steel crumpled under the impact, leaving a fist-size dent.

She put her clothes back on, and thought of another thing to check. She left the public restroom, her hands self-consciously shading her eyes to conceal her weirdness from strangers. Outside a nearby grocery store was a wire rack full of *Breakwater Bulletins*, their pages riffling in the nighttime breeze. She pulled one free and then stuffed it back before retreating to the safety of the public conveniences.

The date was 7 Bloodstone 2003.

Twenty years after it was supposed to be.

As the partygoers had said.

Lukie slumped down on the floor, drawing her knees into her chest.

She needed to remember… everything.

———

"I can't drop you off tonight," Dad said.

"What?" Lukie turned in shock, still in the middle of applying her green eyeshadow. "Dad! This is the most important party ever! This is the last time I'll see everyone!"

"Come to the garage when you're ready." Dad stepped back, leaving Lukie to scowl.

She finished styling her hair. The look was modeled on her favorite bands in the cold wave movement: White Wide Cliffs, Lost Breakfast, and Vizzie Slanter from Outside Sky. Lukie tweaked her eyeshadow one last time, adding another layer of color to make sure it stayed. Picking up her guitar case, she headed for the garage.

And there it was, parked in the driveway. A cherry red Sunjoy sedan, polished and gleaming.

"Happy new car day!" Dad drummed his fingers against the white vinyl roof.

"This is amazing!" Lukie hugged her father hard.

"And you were about to tear my head off!" Dad laughed.

"It's an oldie."

"Only ten years," he said. "It would have been ready last week, but we needed to do a few final tune-ups. Plus, it's a first car. It shouldn't be *new*. You'll need one for Storm City." He cleared his throat.

She gripped him in a big hug and then held out her hands. "Keys?"

Dad removed a key ring from a pocket and dangled it out of reach where she tried to grab it like a cat clawing at a string.

"Some ground rules first," Dad said. "You're home at midnight. No drinking. Remember that guy who just graduated high school and got so drunk he drove off the road and crashed into the Pillars? Don't be like him."

"You know I don't drink," Lukie objected, folding her arms, bangles clanking, annoyed that Dad was bringing up that ancient story yet again.

Dad dropped the keys, and she lunged forward, catching them.

———

Lukie remembered the first feeling of those keys. The weight of them. They felt like freedom. All her hopes and dreams in the palm of her hand. Well, most of them. That car, her wings, her ticket out of Breakwater Bay.

She rocked harder, closed her eyes, and pushed at her memory once more.

CHAPTER 4
THE PARTY

THE PARTY WAS GOING off like a rocket when she drove up the winding road to the Clearwaters' old beach house high on the cliffs. Bass music thumped through the shadowed tree line. The Sunjoy handled well. She'd be able to drive it all the way to university next week with an overnight stop at a motel to charge the battery.

Lukie parked out front on the grassy strip, which was already crowded with sleek electrical motorbikes, big biodiesel SUVs that were popular in the country, and a few sedans like hers. About thirty people would be here tonight, all from school.

She pulled out her guitar case and locked the car.

Nathel's family, the Clearwaters, owned the house. Once the entire area had been part of the Barony of Clearwater, but the last Baron had voluntarily given up his title during the 1930s People's Revolution, announcing that he whole-heartedly believed in Collectivism while also perhaps wanting to avoid being executed by revolutionaries. The Clearwaters had quietly transitioned into becoming rich landowners instead. The beach house was usually rented out to tourists and backpackers, but Nathel's parents allowed him to use it for parties, provided he cleaned up. Those who crashed overnight would find themselves scrubbing the floor or picking up trash the next day, a price some willingly paid.

Lukie entered the house.

The lower story was designed for entertaining. It was an open-plan kitchen, dining, and courtyard area. Upstairs there were bedrooms, but Nathel usually kept those locked. There was less clean-up to do if people stayed downstairs and instead went to the beach or back to their cars for making out. Lukie surveyed the guests—a few hours in and everyone already seemed half-drunk.

"Lead singer's here!" Aspen, the school captain, waved. A ragged cheer and a scattering of applause came from the crowd.

"You're late!" Karra called, appearing from the middle of a crush of dancing teens. Despite the summer heat, she wore a long black dress with lace sleeves. She dripped with bright jewelry, including a silver skull ring that Lukie had given her, all of it carefully chosen to accentuate her dark skin. She gave Lukie a deep kiss and sighed. "You have green stuff every-where again." She had never been fond of Lukie's penchant for over-the-top eyeshadow.

"It's Vizzie Slanter's look!"

"And it's terrible." Karra poked her.

"It's amazing." Lukie wished Karra understood how cool Vizzie was. Time for a topic change. "Guess what? I got a new car! Present from Dad! Listen, is everyone ready for our set?"

"About that," Karra said, a strained smile on her face. "I can't sing tonight."

"And you wait to tell me *now*?" Lukie snapped, her words coming out more harshly than intended. Karra's backing vocals were needed to make the music pop, and more impor-tantly, the new song had been written as a duet. "We were going to debut Crimson Sunrise."

"For fuck's sake, there are more important things that your shitty high school band."

"What's wrong?" Lukie whispered.

"Terek," Karra said. "He's been an absolute pig tonight. Trying to come onto me even when he should know I'm not interested. Calling me a liar and manipulator. I can't pretend to be friends anymore. Let's forget the stupid performance and leave this place. Show me your new car." She leaned forward, red lips pressed close to Lukie's ear. "Please?"

"Hey! Beautiful ladies!" Renwick, the school football champion, staggered past. "Looking forward to Spook Club to rock tonight!" He drunkenly pumped a fist into the air. "Woo!"

"Thanks, Ren!" Lukie waved at him. She had been dreaming of this for weeks. Playing her last, greatest set at the end-of-year party before the class of 1983 headed into the murky world of adulthood, of college or trades or bumming around the beach. Sure, there had been tensions running high in the band, but everyone had promised to put everything aside for their final performance.

Outside, through the open veranda doors, Spook Club was setting up on the deck. Terek on the drums, Nathel with his lead guitar, and Sera with her bass.

"I have to play," Lukie said firmly. "Could you please sing tonight? For me?"

"Can you *not* sing tonight? For me?" Karra countered.

A yawing pit opened in Lukie's stomach. But there was only one way to go.

"I'm going on stage."

"You know, *Lukenaria*, there're more important things to worry about than your stupid music." She wiped at the tears smearing her blue mascara. "Or at least I thought there was." She pulled away, lacy sleeve scraping against Lukie's pleading grip. "Fine, if you won't drive me out of here, I'll call my brother."

Lukie took a deep breath, playing the chorus from Invisible Youth in her head to calm herself. Karra was being so damn selfish. Immeasurable effort had been spent on cajoling the band members to get to this point. It was a promise to their entire cohort. All Karra had to do was put aside her differences for one last performance. But no. *The drama queen.*

For now, the music. Hefting her guitar case, she headed outside.

The sun was setting behind the tangle of pines that hid the dirt road and the nature reserve. Groups gathered, staring out at the darkening eastern sky, at the slate-colored surf that roared against the beach below. Cigarettes glowed like coals, and Lukie smelled pungent alcohols.

"I see you dumped her," Terek called out, walking over to his drum kit. He was a tall, ogre-descended man with heavily freckled skin, protruding brow-ridges, and cavernous eyes. His hair stuck up like a wild bush. "Does this mean you're going to date men again?"

"I go out with whoever I like," Lukie retorted. Sera—she assumed it was the industrious Sera—had already wrangled the amps and wires, taping cables and set lists to the wooden decking.

Lukie opened the guitar case and pulled out her pink Cirrus. Sera helped her connect to an amp.

"Thanks."

Sera nodded, rubbing a sweating hand through her short-cropped red hair. She picked up her bass guitar, carefully tuning it.

"It wouldn't be a Spook Club performance without one of Karra's," Nathel drawled. He was wearing a t-shirt which read 'Fire and dreams and devil dust'—a cryptic reference to the 18th century poet Cadash Moonharp. His hair was dyed a slick black like a raven's wing. He hated his normal golden, metallic shade that marked his descent from the kingdom's ancient nobility. "Finished packing for the Conservatorium?"

"Yes." Lukie said.

"You know that's selling out," Terek laughed.

Maybe Karra was right. He's being a dick tonight, and he promised to behave.

"I want to be a *good* musician," Lukie explained. "Learn theory first. Break it later. Like Vizzie Slanter. There's nothing else like her music."

Terek did a drum roll. "Got my bar business plan sorted. It's the place to be."

Nathel snorted. "You're better off being the next school janitor after old man Peppan. As if anyone would come to a bar you ran. Especially in this crap town."

"As if anyone would want to, with your family here, Baron Clearwater," Terek drawled.

"Shut up! Don't call me that!" Nathel's cheeks burned red.

"Calm down!" Lukie ordered. "We all promised to behave for our final performance." If the band fell apart *now*, the prior weeks of indeterminable practice and pressure would have been for nothing.

"Yeah. This is the last time we have to tolerate each other. Let's stop the chitchat and get this over with." Nathel hunched over his guitar, his black hair flopping over his face.

They had been friends all through high school, but everything had imploded when their final results came through. Lukie and Karra had gotten tertiary education offers in the capital—Storm City. And Sera, Terek, and Nathel hadn't.

Both boys had fumed, fought, and quarreled with everyone. Terek had decided at the last minute to become a local business owner, but Nathel had spent his days brooding.

They had to remain focused on this final performance.

Lukie faced the crowd, hoping that Karra would change her mind, rush up, and join them.

But Karra was nowhere to be seen.

Oh, who needs that song anyway? I can make this work. I don't need her. Lukie leaned into the microphone and said, "Good evening—"

The mike whined with feedback, and Sera frantically came in, adjusting it.

Lukie started again. "Good evening, Breakwater Bay High! Or should I say, free people of Breakwater Bay! No more school. No more rules!"

"Tonight we drool!" Terek shouted.

"Shut up," Lukie growled at him. "Let's play." And her fingers struck the opening chords of Invisible Youth.

————

Lukie, alone in the bathroom in 2003, tried to remember what transpired after that.

She'd performed and…

And that was it. All else was a yawning blur in her mind.

She hadn't figured out anything!

She was somehow dead. Strangled. And had risen as a zombie, like something out of a late-night horror movie.

But why come back after twenty years? Everyone she knew would be old or have moved away.

She needed to find Dad.

But first—

CHAPTER 5
THE HUNT

8:43PM, 7 BLOODSTONE 2003

DUCKING AWAY from the main streets, Lukie perused the silent shopfronts until she found a '$5 store' with a closed sign hanging in the darkened windows. Cheap sunglasses on a spinner rack were near the entrance.

In 1983, they'd only had dollar stores. *Huh. Inflation.*

Lukie punched the door.

She'd meant to break the lock, but instead the entire frame fell inward. Glass shards rained everywhere, and an alarm blared out.

Lukie darted in, grabbed a pair of sunglasses, and fled into the night.

She had snatched the wrong ones. Utterly tasteless, they had yellow frames and daisies on the sides.

A sound of footsteps echoed behind her. Lukie spun around.

No one there.

I'm imagining things.

She hurried home.

———

Lukie's house was opposite the beach, with five cars parked in the driveway, and Dad's collection of surfboards resting against the porch wall. Where the breeze smelled of salt and sand, and where Dad had watched the sea for hours from the old leather chair near the front window.

He was her life's anchor and would figure out everything for her.

But her house was gone.

Instead, there was a *motel*. The 'Sunsurfer,' the sign said. A solid square of brown brick buildings facing a parking lot.

Maybe Dad was in there somehow. Not that he'd ever mentioned wanting to own a motel.

The Sunsurfer blinked its neon sign at her. She skulked toward the reception area and pushed open the door.

An overweight woman behind the desk was engrossed in a television football match. She spoke without looking. "We've got vacancies. Only $60 per night."

Surely Dad hadn't remarried someone like this. "I'm after a man called Zeran Carpenter."

The woman withdrew her attention from the game with a frown of annoyance and squinted at a logbook in front of her. "There's no one of that name checked in."

"He owned the house that was on this block," Lukie insisted. "Before this motel was built."

"Sorry, love. We bought this place ten years ago from a developer." The woman's eyes flicked back to the television.

"Are you sure you don't know Zeran Carpenter at all?" Lukie was tempted to leap over the desk and smash a fist through the screen.

"No. Look, there's a phone book outside." She pointed.

Lukie took the hint and left the woman to her stupid game while heading to the payphone booth on the street corner. The insides of the kiosk were snarled with graffiti. A tattered phone book was jammed in the cabinet under the phone. Lukie pulled it out and flipped through it, hands trembling.

No 'Carpenter, Z' in town.

She stared at the index.

Dad had moved. He hadn't waited.

Why would he? Someone killed me. How do I find out where he went?

But then she recalled the voice. The whispered conversation in the dark.

...you've got until dawn...

Lukie tried to recall *why* she had until dawn. But nothing stirred, no recollections.

She was back from the dead. And had been murdered. She wasn't sure what she was doing here, but years of reading fairy tales and watching horror films told her what she should be doing. And without Dad's help.

She had to find the person who'd strangled her.

Which meant locating someone from the party who would still be around to tell her what had happened over the past twenty years. Someone who wouldn't freak out.

Lukie tore through the phonebook. The Clearwater family was registered, of course, given that they owned half the town. There wasn't a Tanner, S—so Sera was gone. Her parents and brother weren't there, either. No Sailor, K, but Karra's parents were listed at their home address. Terek was still around. She tore out the relevant pages and stuffed them in her jacket.

———

Karra's family lived in 'The Crescent,' an exclusive estate on the edge of the hinterland with its windswept, scrubby grasses and gnarled eucalyptus trees. There, the houses had rested on oversized blocks, with delicate gardens landscaped to allow geomantic energy to flow—or so Karra's mom had always said.

If Karra was still living at home, Lukie would be able to explain herself. Karra believed in ghosts and hauntings.

But when Lukie jogged to a stop in front of Number 12, everything was wrong. A rumble of cars and the glare of headlights indicated that at some point a major road had been built nearby, shattering the solitude of the affluent. And the abodes were rundown, walls and fences scored with graffiti, paint peeling, yards overrun and unkempt.

The once-immaculate garden was full of thigh-high weeds, and the concrete path was cracked. She knocked hesitantly at the door.

She waited and tried again. Eventually, she heard shuffling footsteps inside, and an ancient woman appeared, frail as bird's bones, standing in the dim light. Long gray hair hung past her shoulders.

"Mrs. Sailor?" Lukie barely recognized Karra's mother. Old, so soon. "I..."

Lukie was unprepared for the woman's breakdown. One moment staring at her with a quivering bottom lip, and the next, howling like a stricken beast. A terrible sense of dread settled over Lukie.

Footsteps echoed from within the house, and a huge, balding man appeared.

"What are you doing upsetting my mother?" The man wrapped his arms around the sobbing old lady. She buried her face in his shoulder.

"Sorry," Lukie managed.

"You should be ashamed of yourself!" the man snapped. "Bloody tourists, making a mockery of my sister's murder. Do you think this a joke, for me and my mother? After what we've endured? Get out of here! I'm calling the police."

He slammed the door in her face.

Oh shit.

Two murdered girls. And Karra had been the other one.

The altercation had drawn attention from neighbours. Lights were snapping on, doors were opening and people were coming outside.

Time to look for answers elsewhere.

Lukie fled down the road, colliding with a man in a blue t-shirt standing under a streetlight, and knocking off his baseball cap. The overhead streetlights glinted on his metallic silver hair—a sign of descent from ancient nobility. He was holding a sightseeing map upside down and was staring at her in confusion.

"Sorry!" Lukie mumbled and ran past. Had she seen him before somewhere? The stupid tourists were everywhere.

———

Lukie stopped running when she reached Docker Park. All the familiar equipment—timber and chain-link swings, metal slides—had been replaced by a horrible plastic castle, all tubes, and walkways. It was now only fit for primary school children.

Lukie sat down on a brightly colored plastic seat, clenching her fists.

Karra was dead. She'd been the other murdered girl. But how? She was going to ring Warryn, her older brother, to pick her up. He must have been the man at the door.

So why hadn't he collected her?

What if Karra never got the chance to call?

Lukie twisted her ice-cold hands together. *I had a car. I might have saved her. If only I'd listened. All I wanted to do was play—be the center of attention, the big fish in the little pond.*

Wait, what if Karra's back tonight like I am? She's so much smarter than me. She probably knows who the killer is already. Or she's doing the clever thing and visiting the right people rather than annoying her family. But who could she be investigating?

Well, the obvious suspect was Terek. He'd been a complete dick to everyone since school had ended. Terek was in the phone book, but she knew where he lived. Only she didn't want to risk going to his house. Not if her arrival resulted in the same reaction as her visit to Karra's home.

There was one other place to check first.

Maybe I'll see if he really opened his bar.

CHAPTER 6

THE PLACE TO BE
9:29PM, 7 BLOODSTONE 2003

WHAT HAD ONCE BEEN rows of paint-worn milk bars and bait-and-tackle shops near the old wharf was now a new strip of stylish buildings. Neon lights dazzled her wherever she looked. Strangely dressed tourists in their low-hanging jeans and flattened hair styles wandered along the street in brightly colored shirts and shorts, eating ice creams or sausage rolls. A Blitz Burger restaurant advertized a Surfer Combo with a special Breakwater Brilliant scratch-and-win card, where you could win big prizes from local businesses. All for the exorbitant price of $9.95.

So many hominins. Mostly humans, of course, but there were significant numbers of ogres and dwarrow moving amongst the crowd. No elves. *But they're so stuck up, they wouldn't come here.* She'd learned from her mother that elves preferred their own private communities.

There was only one bar on Main Street. The large neon sign proclaimed it as The Place to Be. And the music pumping from it was That Apocalyptic Feeling by Outside Sky.

That was it.

Hunger gripped her belly. *I'll get a burger later*, she decided. *Wait, if I'm a zombie—*

She tried to imagine eating brains or sucking up blood, but none of those images resonated with her slowly gnawing appetite. Something to worry about after.

Adjusting her stupid sunglasses, she strode into the bar.

Inside, lights strobed and huge televisions played old music clips. It wasn't a large space, but it was densely packed. The décor was standard club: a sticky floor and every other fixture plastic as to be easily wiped down at the end of the night. A mirrored wall ran down one side, partially covered by the bar's counter. Gleaming bottles of different sizes and colors were arrayed on the rear shelf.

The music washed over her. Lukie closed her eyes, remembering how she'd taught herself to play from Vizzie Slanter's songs, reconstructing them on her guitar.

When the Breakout Boys played, Lukie hunted for Terek.

The small dance floor was packed with hominins. Others stood at the edges, drinks resting in front of them on chest-high tables, talking over the noise. Most were human, but she spotted a group of squat, square-shouldered dwarrow at the back of the room. And the people were wearing costumes—faux-school uniforms: shorts or skirts and ties, carrying tennis rackets and stuffed rabbits. Some of their outfits were painted red and torn. A poster on a nearby wall read:

80s Night. Final Night.

7 Bloodstone 1983.

Twenty years ago, two beautiful, innocent schoolgirls were murdered by the Beachside Strangler. The murderer has never been caught. Tonight, we pay our respects with a DANCE and CELEBRATION of their lost lives.

"This is such bad taste," Lukie muttered. She made her

way to the bar—a long marble counter—and tapped her fingers against the cool stone as she tried to see Karra in the crowd.

"Hey, cutie-pie." A voice behind her. "Can I buy you a drink?"

"Terek?" Lukie asked. "Terek Bridgeman?"

Terek was recognizable, but was older and fatter. His crazy crop of hair was now receding and buzz-cut short. He hadn't aged well. Silver chains around his neck and an open-collared shirt made him resemble a gangster. Her first emotion was relief; Terek had survived. And the second was a faint prickling of suspicion and anger. Maybe he knew who the murderer was.

"That's me." He grinned. "But please, Terry's fine. You're a visitor?"

Terek should have recognized her. Even if he was half drunk. They'd grown up together. And Lukie was wearing the same clothes she'd worn to the party; a night that should have stuck in Terek's memory.

But he didn't know her at all.

There is something seriously wrong here. Maybe he's acting. But he's terrible at that. He only got bit parts in the school plays.

"I'm a reporter," Lukie improvised. "Sukie Smith. From Storm City. Doing a write-up on regional events."

"I can tell you everything that goes on here," Terek promised. He gestured to the well-trained barman who quickly produced two glasses. The first was a beer, and the second, a large cocktail with a little paper umbrella, which he pushed into her hands with such confidence that Lukie suspected it was an old habit. "This is my bar."

At least one of her friends had achieved their dream.

"I'd like to know about this Final Night."

Terek laughed and took a long swig of beer. "The only interesting thing that happened around here."

"But weren't two girls murdered? Isn't throwing a party on the anniversary of their deaths in bad taste?" She recalled the furious glare in Warryn's eyes as he slammed the door in her face.

"Nah." Terek wiped his lips with his sleeve. "If it wasn't for the parties, the average punter in this town would have forgotten their names by now. By doing this, we're keeping their memories alive. And for the twentieth anniversary, we've got people from all over the continent arriving. Good for the economy. We're not completely heartless—there's a big service in the church tonight. Candles and stuff. Everyone has different ways of coping with grief. Take your pick, party or prayer."

"Did you know the girls personally?"

Terek shook his head. "Not really. I was a teenage boy. Into football, cars, that sort of thing. The two of them would never have talked to someone like me." His voice was edged with bitterness.

Lukie worried if she'd completely crossed over into a parallel timeline. One where Terek had never spoken to her or joined the band.

But why am I dead? He must know something. He must.

"Did you go to that last party?" Lukie tried to sip the cocktail, but it was like sucking down gasoline. *Wait, why can't I drink this? That is so strange.* Her stomach churned uncomfortably. *I'm starving. What the hell do I eat?* She pretended to swallow.

Terek shrugged. "I did, but can barely remember it. Must have been off my face on beer or weed. The police spoke to all of us kids at the party, but no one knew anything. I kept saying it had to be a stranger, but they didn't listen. Wasted a lot of time." He sighed and stepped forward into her personal space, and his hand lightly brushed her wrist. For a second, she heard music and her stomach rumbled: 1970s heavy metal, all bitterness and frustration.

The music had come from Terek; not from the bar's speakers that were now playing Powerhouse by the Magpie Twins. Like that blast of dance funk that had burst out of nowhere when Maz had brushed against her. *I hear music when I touch people? What does that mean? It's making me so hungry.*

She licked her cold lips and stepped back.

"A stranger?" she repeated.

"Yeah, we get lots of backpackers and tourists." Terek waved his glass. "They're here for a few days and gone the next. Nothing much we can do about it but remember the girls through stuff like this. Do you want to dance?"

An uncomfortable feeling seized Lukie. Behind her, the young silver-haired man with the tourist t-shirt was leaning against the counter, regarding her with a cool and unblinking gaze.

"Hey, you at least fucking look at me after I bought you that cocktail," Terek snapped, following her line of sight.

He gripped her shoulder and the rage of his music filled Lukie.

Without thinking, she locked her hand around Terek's arm.

And drank from him.

CHAPTER 7
CAGE

9:50PM, 7 BLOODSTONE 2003

LUKIE WAS FEEDING. The sound of clashing drumbeats —the chorus of Terek's life—overwhelmed her. On one hand, he'd achieved his post-high school dream and opened the most popular bar in town. But his success hadn't bought him the popularity he craved. People still thought of him as a thug because of his ogre blood, despite his successful business. And the small town gossip obsessed him and worried at him like flea bites, souring him from within. As Lukie guzzled Terek's essence, she saw him arguing with a parade of girlfriends. Buying expensive cars and smashing the windows of rival businesses with bricks; becoming the stereotype that he'd desperately tried to avoid.

Part of Lukie was conscious that whatever she was eating, it included Terek's memories. Instinctively, she sought out what he'd seen that night.

But there wasn't anything there. Just a dull, eaten-out hollow. His recall of school and the party was a fog. He knew names and people, enough to get by, but most of it was gone.

There had to be a clue *some*where. She drank faster until…

A moment later, Lukie crashed against the mirrored wall behind the bar, breaking shelves and shattering glass. She scrambled to her feet, then leaped onto the counter, trying to figure out what had happened and why she hadn't finished draining Terek.

The silver-haired man. He was between her and Terek, and it was very clear to Lukie that he'd thrown her across the room. Her mind hissed with blank static. Did this man have soul music like Terek and Maz, or was he something else? Whatever he was, his spiritual interference wasn't the slightest bit appetizing.

She needed more of Terek, who was lying so conveniently on the floor. And the inedible silver-haired guy was in the way.

"Leave," the man commanded the crowd who'd stopped drinking and dancing to stare. His hands flicked about in a complicated motion, and when he released them, a glowing symbol hung in the air for a few seconds.

At once, bar patrons fled.

What the—?

Terek shambled past, following the fleeing people. Unable to control herself, Lukie dove off the bar at him.

But then the silver-haired man intercepted her and deflected her charge with a ducking, twisting movement. Lukie hit the floor head-first, crashing into sticky pools of beer and broken glasses. Static hissed at the back of her mind. Her fingers clenched in frustration.

The man gestured with his right hand, and a glowing golden sword appeared in it, giving off little motes of stray light like a birthday sparkler.

Although she was still driven by hunger, she was able to regain a modicum of restraint. *I need to run.*

She scrambled backward as the man swept his shining blade at her. She rolled away and leapt up. Something hit the floor.

Hah! He missed! On her feet now, she ran for the exit, only to collide with an invisible barrier that was between her and the wall. She punched at the air in frustration, but her fingers slipped off a slick surface that shouldn't have been there.

The man walked toward her, sword in one hand and holding a photograph in the other.

Lukie frantically patted her pockets. The left side of her jacket was slashed open. Her last family photo wasn't there.

"Give that back," she roared.

He shook his head.

The picture was important beyond its sentimental value. She couldn't describe how or why, but she needed it. A wave of fury washed over her, and she charged.

He slid to the right like a dance move. Unable to halt her momentum, Lukie crashed into tables, half-full beer glasses falling on her. She flailed around, got up. This was a bad idea. But it was difficult to convince herself of that. A big part of her wanted to fight things, drink peoples' essences, and not care about the long-term consequences.

What's wrong with me?

The silver-haired man pointed the golden sword at her face. Fizzy motes of light sparked off its end. "Don't move."

The man pulled a device from his belt: a slender walkie talkie. "Detective? It's Cage. I've got a newly risen revenant. One of the dead girls from '83, I believe."

He sketched a shape in the air above her with his left hand, still holding the photo. Then he stepped away, whistling.

Lukie tried to rise, but the invisible walls pressed around her. She pushed and kicked but was unable to get up. "What did you do to me?"

Cage went behind the bar and began placing the intact bottles on the counter. "A simple ward. It won't be long."

"Let me go!" Lukie demanded.

"Not yet." Cage picked up a cocktail shaker and scrutinized the collection of alcohols. "You haven't left me a lot to work with. Hmmm. A Blue Sunrise, perhaps, if I can find some pineapple juice."

A stocky man squeezed through the bar doors. He wore a sweat-stained white dress shirt. A police badge hung around his neck on a silver chain. His red hair was graying, and he had a thick mustache. When he saw Lukie, his mouth opened.

She also recognized him—Sera's brother, Arnel Tanner. He'd been a much better older brother to Sera than Warryn had been to Karra; letting his little sister borrow the car whenever they needed to get to gigs.

Sera, please be around somewhere…

"You look like a fish, Detective." Cage was squinting at labels. "Be careful. There's broken glass everywhere."

"Lukie?" the man whispered, coming to where she was struggling against the invisible barrier. "You're... you're alive..."

"Nope. She's dead." Cage held up a bottle of brandy. "Undead, to be precise."

"I'm not dead, you asshole." Lukie punched at the unseen wall. "Give me my photograph!" It was getting hard to focus again. She needed to feed—she hadn't gotten enough from Terek.

"It'll have to be a Blue Horizon," Cage mused. "No pineapple juice." He jiggled the shaker at the detective.

"I won't ask why you're making cocktails after a bar fight," the detective muttered.

Lukie watched him crunch through the broken glass and sticky pools of beer toward her. "Arnel! What's happening? What happened to Sera?"

The detective's cheeks reddened. He scratched at his mustache.

"Uh, well." He cleared his throat. "This might be a lot to take in, but—"

While part of her wanted to listen to him, her feral zombie instincts betrayed her. She threw herself against the invisible wall like a shark against a cage, desperate for his essence.

"Detective!" Cage called while pouring various liquids into the shaker. "Let the revenant feed from you."

"My blood?" the detective asked. "For Lukie, anything." He slipped a pen knife from his pocket.

"She's not a vampire." Cage sighed. "She's a revenant. They eat souls."

"Wait, *souls*?" Lukie managed.

"Aaaah." The detective stepped away. "Don't people need their souls?"

"It's your memories and essence," Cage said. "Your spiritual imprint. Without identity, we're nothing. Think of a recollection you don't need. Nothing foundational. Imagine it as a photograph separate from you. Touch the girl and then visualize yourself giving her the picture. Keep your thoughts focused. Yes, it will wound you, but you'll recover in time. When she's satiated, I'll help her. She'll be much easier to reason with."

The detective took a deep breath. "I wish this was yesterday when I didn't believe in any of this supernatural stuff." He reached his hand forward, pushing through the invisible wall. Lukie grabbed it hungrily. Music washed over Lukie. While Terek had been clanging drums, this man was a mournful cello solo. Images flashed, and she slurped them down.

He was seven years old and sitting in the stalls of the boys' toilets in a shopping center. His heart was hammering, but being here was important. He belonged here.

Then a cruel woman's voice cut through his inner peace.

"Sera, get out of the men's toilets," his mother said.

He pulled up his pants and opened the door. Her hand gripped his wrist tightly. "You're not a boy," she scolded. Men were standing around, staring at them in bemusement. "You're such an embarrassment. The other mothers keep laughing at me at the bowling club." She dragged him outside, and he burst into tears...

The man pulled back. Lukie felt full, like she'd just finished eating one of Dad's roast dinners.

"Sera? That's you?"

The beefy man nodded, cheeks colored with red. "It's Tamlyn now."

Lukie got up to embrace him but crashed into the barrier.

"Can you let me out?" she asked Cage. "I'm not crazy anymore."

Cage snapped his fingers.

Lukie poked at the air in front of her like a mime in an imagined prison. Her hands cut through empty space. She got up and gave Tamlyn a measured hug.

"So cold," Tamlyn said, shaking her off after a few seconds, shivering.

"I ate your memory," Lukie said. "Is it really gone?"

"I'm sure it was something I can live without," Tamlyn said, righting two chairs at one of the tall tables. They sat. "The more important thing is, are you okay? You're not going to attack anyone else?"

"I'm good." Lukie rubbed at her stomach. Her thoughts were clear and the horrible craving was gone. "But what if I get hungry again?"

"You should be all right for a while." Cage smirked. Golden light faded away around him. Like he'd done something that she hadn't been aware of. He slid the photo into his jeans pocket.

Giving the weirdo a quick glare, Lukie focused on her old friend. "You became a *man*? Did you know at school you were going to?"

"Yeah."

"But you never told me." Hadn't all those years of schooling and growing up with each other meant anything?

Tamlyn sighed. "I was the glue holding our crazy group together. I didn't want you to know about my problems. I was the strong, silent one."

Lukie remembered Sera in school. Quiet, dependable. The person who always got things done. Who carried peace messages between Karra and Lukie when they'd quarreled, who'd kept the boys from fighting too loudly. *Did I take her for granted? Did I ever ask if she had any problems or wanted to talk about anything private? I guess she hid it so well.*

Tamlyn handed her a handkerchief. "You've got glass on your face."

She took it from him and wiped away splinters.

"I was going to tell you before you left for the Conservatorium, but you were gone."

"I'm sorry—"

"Let's continue this reunion later," Cage called out. He poured a lurid purple cocktail into a martini glass, sipping it delicately. "Not bad. I'll make you something, Detective. You need a drink."

"Pour me a beer."

"No, you're on duty," Cage said. "A strawberry mocktail."

"Whatever." Tamlyn gritted his teeth. He loomed over Lukie, placing his hands on her shoulders gently. "This is important because it's not every day we get victims returning from the dead. Tell me everything you know about the person who killed you."

CHAPTER 8
SOME KIND OF MONSTER
11:04PM, 7 BLOODSTONE 2003

TAMLYN'S unmarked police car slid through the night. The detective gripped the wheel, shoulders hunched. To her surprise, Lukie had been allowed to sit in the front. Cage lounged in the back, rubbing at a stack of scratch-and-win cards with a small coin.

The cello music—the taste of Tamlyn's soul—faintly reverberated in her mind, so unlike the rough bashing of Terek's drums. But the notes were laced with a discordant rhythm that sank into her consciousness like acid, dissolving something primal within.

"Are you feeling okay?" Tamlyn asked.

"I'm dead. What do you think?" She stared out the window into the dark streets and poked at the car's stereo system. A good hit of 80s rock would wash away the cello. "Where's the cassette deck?"

"We've got CDs now. Glovebox."

"Do you have any Outside Sky? Did Vizzie release any new albums?" She opened the compartment in front of her and pulled out an assortment of square cases enclosing silver discs. So futuristic! She was shocked at the covers which showed a plethora of singers in broad-brimmed hats clutching acoustic guitars. "Country music? What happened to you?"

"Two of my best friends were murdered," Tamlyn said crisply.

She slammed the glove box shut and stared out the window. She didn't feel like talking about music anymore.

"Where's Dad?"

"Moved away," Tamlyn said. "Not sure where. Most people took the developers' cash and relocated. The town boomed. Only Nathel and Terek remain from our high school cohort. It's just the old folk. Terek stayed because he wanted to—saw dollar signs—and Nathel… well, he didn't seem to want to do anything."

"But where did he go? C'mon, Se—Tamlyn, you must have some idea."

He just shook his head. "He up and left. Lukie, he wasn't the same after you—you know. He didn't trust anyone anymore. He hassled the cops back then until they turned on him. Your father started drinking—"

Drinking? That wasn't like Dad at all. Lukie swallowed the ball of sadness threatening to choke her. "I'm guessing the murders fucked everything up?"

"To put it mildly." Tamlyn never took his eyes off the road. "The entire town changed overnight. No one trusted anyone. Accusations rattled around like a bag full of marbles. Nothing was proven."

"When I find the guy who killed me, I'll rip off his face." Lukie clenched her fists.

"No, we'll take them into custody," Tamlyn said. "Whoever it was—man or woman—has to go to court. Everyone needs to know what they've done."

"Why haven't you solved the murder yet?" Lukie demanded.

"Not enough evidence. And you might remember you've

been dead twenty years—this is a very cold case, and cold cases don't get priority," Tamlyn said. "And I was a teenager struggling with the death of my friends before years of transitioning, becoming a cop. Things take time, Lukie."

"And why is he here?" Lukie jerked her head in Cage's direction.

"I am fortune's knight," Cage explained. "Fate guides me to the world's wounds. Where the boundaries between the mundane and supernatural realms weaken. And where I can make a difference."

"You randomly visit a place, and things go wrong?" Lukie mocked.

"They're usually wrong before I get here."

"It must be like living in a TV show," Tamlyn mused. "Like the Steel Deputy. Remember that show, Lukie? He'd drive into a new town where a kidnapping was going on or a gang was holding everyone hostage. And he'd shoot down the baddies with his car lasers."

"It was on last night." A pang for the times when she'd sit down and watch the television with Dad stabbed her. "My time."

"I was hoping to hit the beach before the weirdness began." Cage plucked at his tourist t-shirt. "Perhaps afterwards."

"So how did you get the cops helping you?" Lukie demanded.

"I can be persuasive when I have to be. The chief graciously offered me the services of the good detective for a day or two. It's always best to work with the local authorities. I try to give them a heads-up when I arrive in town that something bad might happen. I went out for a burger and saw you survive the car crash. Followed you. Learned you were one of the girls that came back."

"Where's Karra?" Lukie bit her lip. "She must be wandering around like me."

"I didn't see any other revenants."

"Maybe we'll find her," Tamlyn said. "But let's work together for now. What do you remember?"

"Nothing." Lukie scowled. "It's a blur in my mind. How come you're not more freaked out that I'm here as a zombie?

"I am freaked out, Lukie." Tamlyn's face was a blank mask focused on the road ahead. "I thought Cage was crazy when he said something supernatural was going to happen. But it's not so bad now. I mean, it's *you*. Even if you are a zombie, it's great to be able to see and talk to you again."

"She's a revenant, not a mindless eater of brains," Cage interrupted from the back seat. Lukie twisted around. He was looking down, still working his way through his stack of scratch-and-win cards. He held up the most recent one, frowned and tossed it to one side. "*Not* a zombie."

"Lukie, put your seatbelt on," Tamlyn said.

"Why?" she snapped. "It's not like I'll *die*."

"I could lose my license," Tamlyn murmured.

"Revenant 101. Tell me about myself." Lukie relented and strapped in. "Aren't you scared I'll drink your soul?"

"You're satiated." Cage selected a new card from the pile beside him. "You shouldn't need anything else for a while."

"But if I do?" she challenged.

"You won't get far." Cage smiled, his words a mild threat.

"*How* did I come back?" Lukie asked. "Where was I for twenty years?"

"You were in Tenebra. The Underworld. A miserable place full of ghosts that devour each other to survive."

"That's not right!" Lukie hunched forward. Something stirred, a memory again, of running but not along the beach, somewhere dark. "What about the Precursor's Garden?" *Where Mom is. Waiting for me.* "Everyone's supposed to go there when they die. I've never heard of Tenebra."

"The afterlife is a fractured, dangerous affair," Cage said. "Not everyone can travel to the paradise realms. Those who fall to the Underworld are those consumed by their regrets and passions. The greatest are the ghost lords, who build entire labyrinthine cities of their lost desires. They empower other spirits—selfish, obsessed creatures—to walk the living lands as their monstrous servants. Those are the revenants, vessels for their masters' desperate passions."

"Lukie isn't a monster," Tamlyn interrupted. "And selfish and obsessed? Have you met any teenagers lately?"

Lukie's head whirled. Cage's words reminded her of some dark place.

Shadowy tendrils coming after her.

Fleeing through gloomy corridors.

And then, out of nowhere, stairs leading up to a closed apart-ment door.

Light trickling through a crack.

"I'm not a monster," Lukie whispered.

"Then what was the bargain you struck with your master? What did you agree to do for them in exchange for your unlife?" Cage frowned at his card. "I've got twenty percent off boat hire. I was hoping for the burger combo." He flung it to one side.

All Lukie remembered was screaming at someone, begging them for aid, less negotiation than a hostage situation.

"I... Uh..." Lukie trailed off. "I can't remember."

"You can't recall the most important decision you've ever made? The entire crux of your undead existence?" Cage prodded.

"No!" she snapped, folding her arms.

Cage shook his head.

"Wait, I have until dawn to hunt the killer," she blurted. *I think.* "I woke up at dusk—what time is it now?"

"About eleven," Tamlyn said. "Sunrise is at five."

Only six hours left? That soul-craving had completely ruined her focus. "I have to get out of this car and find them!" She twisted in her seat, reaching for the handle.

"You'll need our help." Tamlyn's tone didn't change. "I know this place and Cage knows about supernatural stuff."

"But what happens if we don't locate the bastard by dawn?" Lukie slumped. "I turn into dust?"

In the rearview mirror, she saw Cage give a quick shrug. "It depends on the bargain you made."

He picked up another scratch-and-win card. "Look, let's focus on finding the killer for now. Tell us what you remember. Even if it's just fragments."

She described saying goodbye to Dad, driving to the party. Her clash with Karra, and then playing with the band.

"Anything else?"

"Uh, everything after that is hazy. Where are we going?" She peered at the passing scenery, trying to figure it out. But too much time had gone by, and the landmarks were wrong.

"Beach house," Tamlyn said.

"Really? *Why?* It's in ruins. There's nothing there."

"It's where you died and came back." Cage finished his card and sighed, dropping it and picking up another one. "It might be important."

He doesn't have any idea, does he? Maybe he is telling the truth. He just wanders around until he stumbles into something supernatural. What a fool. She wanted to throw a country music CD at him, but stopped herself. He'd already humiliated her once.

And I'm not a monster. I can't be.

But all she could think of was Terek fleeing from her as she hungered for his soul.

CHAPTER 9

THE SHADOW WORLD

THEY TOOK the paved road and then the gravel drive to the beach house. The headlights illuminated a collection of maybe thirty parked cars. Music boomed from portable cassette decks—or whatever they used nowadays—and the sounds of shouting people rang out from within the ruins.

For a few seconds, Lukie hoped they'd found 1983 again. But the vehicles were mostly the strange ones from 2003, and the current song had an incredibly quick tempo.

"Trespassers," Tamlyn swore as he pulled up. "They're not supposed to be here. The structure might collapse on top of them."

"Why hello, Detective," someone drawled, and a man with shaggy metallic-blonde hair stepped into the headlights, smiling crookedly. His black t-shirt was emblazoned with the logo: 'Outside Sky: The Midnight Justice Tour.' It reminded Lukie that she had no idea what had happened to her favorite bands. "This is private property. And not *your* private property."

Nathel. Physically, he was the least changed of Lukie's old friends. Older, but more late twenties than forty. Yet there was something about him—an inexplicable weight that Tamlyn and Terek lacked.

Tamlyn got out of the car. "Sorry, mate, I didn't think you'd be here. Haven't seen you around for ages. When was the last time you left the mansion?"

Nathel swallowed, quivering.

"If there's anything you want to tell me, you can." Tamlyn's tone was warm and earnest.

Lukie slipped out of the car's passenger side, eager to talk to her old friend.

Nathel rubbed at his forehead. "I..." Then he stopped, stared for a few heartbeats at Lukie, then fled into the thick trees that bordered the old property.

"Wait!" Tamlyn yelled, but he was accosted by a dwarrow in a sundress: one of the twenty-somethings who had been in the car that had run over her earlier.

"Hey, he said you were a detective. I'm Juta Stonehall. Our friends Gerron and Maz are missing. They went off into the woods to make out but haven't come back yet." She burped. "They get like dumb teenagers when they drink, especially after free beers. But it's been too long, and no one's answering their phone."

Tamlyn listened to the dwarrow woman continue her statement. Lukie moved to join him, but Cage raised a hand in the air. "Let the detective deal with the situation. You can help us more if you learn to use your powers."

"I have powers?"

"Yes. Everything within you flows from Tenebra," Cage explained, leading her to the ruin. "The Underworld."

Lukie thought of the dark smoke that had oozed out of her after her car accident early that evening. *Is that all that's in me now? Darkness, not blood.*

They cut through the little camps of partygoers that

surrounded the old house. It wasn't a cohesive single party—rather like a wild outdoor music concert. Teenagers rolled on picnic blankets, people danced or trawled their portable coolers for beer while others leapt up and down, displaying varied skills at dancing.

"What you're going to do is use this place as a touchstone." Cage pointed to the open shell in the distance, its frames blotting out the cloud of stars overhead. "By using the location and your connection to Tenebra, you might be able to recall more than you can now."

They stood in front of the house. A line of yellow tape warned people from entering. Ignoring the instructions, a small group danced on the cracked, weed-infested slab. Like her high school class had done twenty years ago.

"Why don't you do it?" Lukie waved her fingers in the air, sketching one of the glyphs that Cage had demonstrated earlier. "You can make gold sparkly things."

"I'm not a revenant." Cage answered. "Still alive."

"Not helpful." Lukie folded her arms. "You want my assistance, tell me about yourself."

"I'm a preserver." Cage ducked under the line of yellow plastic tape, gesturing at her to follow him. "An ordinary man gifted a modicum of powers to stop the supernatural from threatening the innocent." He frowned slightly like he didn't believe his own words.

"But how can this be real?" Lukie tugged at her hair. "I was told all my life that the magic is gone. How come no one knows about this stuff?"

Cage shook his head. "There are ancient rituals and pacts that keep magical knowledge hidden from the mundane. The Rending, the spell which ended the age of magic, was intended to seal all magic and monsters away in their home dimensions. Yet the Rending was imperfect. There are cracks in the world which mortals might stumble upon to strike a bargain with an other-dimensional entity. The patron imbues their protege with a vestige of themselves, and the mortal gains occult powers. My patron is a fallen hero who gave their life for a cause. Your patron is one of the ghostly sovereigns of Tenebra. Most revenants I've encountered are crazed things, driven to slake an endless craving for what they—and their patron—lost from life."

"I'm not a monster." Lukie scowled. *And who the hell is my patron?* She scratched at her chest. There wasn't anything within her that felt *other. Why would some all-powerful ghost help out a murdered teen? Why did I agree?*

"I'm giving you a chance to prove it." Cage led her to a corner of the cracked concrete slab away from the dancers. Strings of festival lights glittered from atop the broken walls. Brown grass weeds thrust up through the cracks. The nighttime ocean wind cut in from the sea, and its biting chill didn't make Lukie feel any less cold or dead.

"It will be easier to channel your power with one of your artifacts." He pulled her photograph out of his jeans pocket, holding it up.

"Give me that!" Lukie reached for it. Her fingers lightly grazed Cage's hand only for him to slip away from her grasp as though he was on ice skates. A crackle and hiss blurred through her mind.

"And why does your soul music sound like static?"

"A precaution," Cage said. "And music, eh? The last revenant I met thought souls tasted like different wines. Don't ask after his health. Anyway, use one of the other artifacts I left you."

He's so annoying. But he knew how things worked, which was more than she did. Lukie unzipped her jacket pocket and retrieved the car keys. They were comforting to hold. "What do these do?"

"Those objects are the embodiments of the memories that kept you sane in Tenebra," Cage explained. "The anchors of your existence."

"And assholes like you can use them against me," Lukie snapped.

"If I hadn't intervened in the bar, that man—your old friend—would have died. I could have killed you there like a monster, but I gave you a chance. Don't make me regret it. I hate being wrong." Cage stared over her head. He rarely made eye contact. "Focus on your artifact. Call upon the realm of shadows, find an echo within it, a deeper layer that holds the key to your final night."

Lukie fingered her keys. She remembered more of Tenebra now that Cage had reminded her. Dream-like hungry things with blank faces. Running through tunnels. She held up her car keys, not sure how to use them. *Wait, it's all about memories?*

She imagined her Sunjoy as it had been last night, or twenty years ago. She opened the door, smelled polished leather. She sat in the driver's seat, hit the brake, and turned the ignition. Just how Dad had taught her. An overwhelming sense of powerlessness and regret flooded her, and with that lonely emotion, she unlocked the shadow world.

Cage had said the other realms were sealed away. Through a barrier that felt more like bulging plastic sheeting than a wall, she perceived Tenebra, an ocean of darkness just on the other side. Black velvet waves pushed against the partition between worlds. Whispering sirens called her into the depths.

No, the party. I'm going to remember the party.

The gloom parted for her as she reached out. Tiny fragments of memory in smoked glass bottles were carried upon bleak tides like flotsam. Endless dancing, beating music, late night talking and drinking.

The waters pulled back further, revealing a shadow image of the beach house.

She stepped forward into it.

And then all around her, 1983 came to life.

The night she died.

CHAPTER 10
ONCE MORE, WITH FEELING

11:42PM, 7 BLOODSTONE 2003

LUKIE STEPPED out of the Sunjoy sedan. The rich, salty smell of the ocean filled the air. She quickly pressed two fingers against her neck and felt a racing pulse and warm skin. Alive again, 1983.

This time, everything would go perfectly.

She didn't bother with her guitar, instead, she raced for the beach house.

"Lead singer's here!" Aspen called out as Lukie banged the door open. A ragged cheer and a scattering of applause came from the crowd.

"You're late!" Karra drifted toward her, dress flowing like dark seafoam. She gave Lukie a deep kiss.

Lukie grabbed her lost girlfriend, kissed her deeply and then took her by the hand.

"What brought this on?" Karra wiped the tears from Lukie's face. "Now there's green stuff smeared everywhere."

"It's been so long since I last saw you." Lukie rubbed at her eyes, not caring about smudges. It had only been last night since she'd last seen Karra—in her subjective time—but it still felt like a thousand years had passed. "I said all the wrong things. I didn't listen. I'm sorry."

"I don't remember, but who cares." Karra held her tight. "I can't sing tonight."

"I know." Lukie gripped Karra's hand. "We'll perform another time. Let's go for a drive in my new car. You can tell me everything."

Ignoring the shouts from Nathel, she led Karra outside under the shadows of the pine trees where the bright yellow face of the moon gleamed. She pulled open the Sunjoy's door—

————

—and found herself crouching on a cracked concrete slab. The broken frames of the house reared up against the stars. Cage shone the flashlight into her eyes. Her heart was still; she remained dead.

"The vision stopped!" she raged. "I was about to save her!"

"It's not real." Cage stamped on the ground. "You're using this place and your connection with Tenebra to assist your recollections. You can't change what's occurred, only view it."

"Oh… this sucks so bad." She could still feel Karra's lips pressing against hers.

"Find out what happened," Cage instructed. "Don't rewrite the script. Just live within it."

Frustrated, Lukie closed her eyes, feeling the sea of shadows draw her into its gloomy embrace—

————

Lukie stepped out of her Sunjoy sedan, smelling the salty air. She was alive again, but this time, she felt no joy in it.

Because she had to stick to the script. Repeat the same shitty decisions that she'd already made.

She trudged to the door, guitar case in hand. Pushed it open.

"Lead singer's here!" Aspen called.

"You're late!" Karra floated over.

"Hey." Lukie savored one last kiss. She'd come back from the dead, and magic and monsters were real. So there had to be a way to return to 1983 and do everything right.

"You've got green stuff everywhere again," Karra pointed out.

"Yeah." What else had she said? "Oh, I have a new car. Um, it's red."

"Listen," Karra said. "I can't sing tonight."

"I need to play," Lukie mumbled, hefting her guitar case.

"For fuck's sake, there are more important things than your shitty garage band," Karra snapped. "One last request. Let's get away from this horrible party. Drive me anywhere you like in your new car."

"I'm sorry." Lukie wiped her face. "I have to play tonight."

"You and *your* stupid music." Karra turned and vanished into the crowd.

But it was always our *music, wasn't it?*

Watching her go, heart racing, Lukie walked through the house to where the band was setting up.

The evening sunset colored the sky in stripes of gold and lavender. Friends from school moved around her, calling greetings, patting her on the back, but she ignored them.

"I see you dumped her." Terek drummed a sting: *ba-boom tsh!* "Or she dumped you. Does this mean you're going to start dating men again?"

"No." Lukie opened her guitar case and pulled out her pink Cirrus, sorting through cables that trailed across the floor. Sera helped her connect to an amp.

"Thanks," Lukie said.

Sera nodded and picked up her bass guitar. Lukie wished she had somehow noticed the pain that Sera must have been going through back then. But she couldn't do anything about that now.

"It wouldn't be a Spook Club performance without one of Karra's," Nathel drawled.

"Shut up, Nathel," Lukie snarled. "I want to play tonight. No chit chat." She strummed the opening chords of 'Invisible Youth,' and the crowd roared.

She lost herself quickly in the set, performing with anger and regret. Everyone cheered and clapped more than they usually did at these drunken parties.

Hey, I've skipped beyond the blank! she thought, triumphant.

"Got you a drink," Nathel murmured during a break, handing her an already open can of Thunder Cola.

"You're the best." Lukie said with a grin. "Sorry for snapping at you earlier. Let's rock this place!"

She drank deeply and played the second half of their set. She didn't bother with Crimson Sunrise and performed Invisible Youth twice instead.

Everything got *weird* as the music continued. She kept giggling. Missing notes and chords. The world blurred.

And then there was a gap. A bonfire. Sparks drifting into the night sky to join the thousands of stars overhead.

Another gap.

She was standing on the beach. The midnight waves washed over her feet like a warning caress. Her head fogged, and she had trouble staying upright. Above, the full moon was visible, and the thin, planetary ring gleamed like stones on a bracelet.

What's wrong with me? She fell into the lapping waters.

"No!"

Back to the real world with Cage standing over her. Music from the partygoers banged away in the background.

"I can't remember," Lukie fumed. "I couldn't see who killed me. And I don't know what happened to Karra!"

"Did you—" he whipped his head around, staring into the pine trees in the distance. "The detective is in danger!"

CHAPTER 11
THE SILHOUETTE

12:00AM, 7 BLOODSTONE 2003

TAMLYN! Lukie had just found one of her old friends. And she wasn't going to lose him again.

Cage pointed at the dark line of pine trees in the distance that pushed against the sky like blackened spears.

Without waiting for further guidance, she ran outside the ruined house and onto the grass beyond, knocking over music players, sending bottles skittering, bashing aside drink coolers, and crashing through groups of confused partygoers who shouted and screamed after her.

But Lukie didn't care about the havoc in her wake. She had to get to the forest fast.

Overhead, the cloud of stars above was partially concealed by pointed branches. The ring's light glinted like a knife blade.

And she stopped because she had no idea where to go next. "Tamlyn!" she yelled out. "Where are you?"

Footsteps behind her crunched over pine needles. But it was only Cage, slightly out of breath. A small flashlight glowed in his hands, even though there was plenty of natural illumination. He moved his head back and forth like a dog sniffing for a scent. Cage flipped a coin in one hand, then abruptly headed east through the trees toward the ocean.

He better not be picking a direction at random.

In a clearing further on, the overhead light exposed two shapes.

Tamlyn, being dragged over a sticky trail of blood-soaked pine needles. And the thing taking him away—a perfect silhouette, moving with a heavy limp.

Lukie ran forward. "Let go of him!"

The shape obeyed and dropped Tamlyn.

Barreling ahead, Lukie slammed into the creature, colliding with slick, oozing meat. Its fleshy padding absorbed her blow.

Huge hands gripped her neck and crushed it. A deep rhythmic baritone voice, singing nonsense, filled her mind: *bop, do-wop, bop, bop, bop, bom, bom, bop...*

"You came back for more? So pathetic." The voice was like scraping steel. And terribly familiar.

She couldn't move.

She remembered.

Ice-cold hands squeezing her throat. Not being able to breathe. Flailing wildly, trying to scream for help, but nothing coming from her mouth. Being dragged along the shore, tidal waves lapping at her ankles. Getting weaker, spots dancing before her eyes, gasping and blacking out.

She snapped back to awareness a few seconds later, clawing at her throat.

The monster had released her, and Cage was in front of it. His sword shifted from golden light to the color of greasy smoke, and he lunged forward, striking the shadowy figure.

It made a terrible, rasping growl and retreated.

Cage moved in again, slashed. Slipped left, cut. "Get him to safety!"

Lukie ducked over to Tamlyn and hefted him. *It's a good*

thing I've got this super zombie strength. Trusting Cage to hold off the *thing,* she lugged the detective out of the pine forest and back to his car. To her relief, Tamlyn was conscious. He slumped in the driver's seat, coughed, and pulled a handkerchief from his pocket to wipe the blood and dirt off his face.

"Are you okay?" Lukie still felt those monstrous hands wrapped around her neck, the chill burning like liquid nitrogen.

"Yeah," Tamlyn wheezed.

Fear made her undead stomach churn. "That was it. That was the thing that murdered me and Karra. And I have no idea what it was or who it was." And she hadn't been able to do anything at all while she relived her murder.

"Go help Cage," Tamlyn ordered.

"But it just about crushed me! Again!"

Tamlyn placed a trembling hand on her arm. "You came back to deal with this thing, whatever it is."

"But Cage can handle it! He's a hero right out of a TV show."

"Listen to me," Tamlyn said. "We need to make sure this monster is stopped. Tonight. He took those two kids. Dragged them away into a hole in the ground. Help Cage save them. You said you only have until dawn. If that's all the time you have, you'd better use it well."

Lukie twitched, but he was right. She needed to confront the shadow.

"You drive out of here," Lukie said. "Get somewhere safe. Don't hang around."

"I'll radio for help." Tamlyn fumbled for his keys and sat in the driver's seat.

"It was good to see you again." Lukie sprinted toward the treeline before she heard his response. She hoped that when she returned to the clearing, she would find Cage sitting on the monster's hacked-up corpse, flipping his coin, or furiously rubbing at another scratch-and-win card. But all was quiet.

"Cage?" she called out.

Whispers drew her forward. A hole in the ground pooled like ink. The voices beckoned her. It was horribly familiar, like revisiting a place that she'd hated as a child.

Tenebra.

A direct portal to the Underworld. A raw wound on the earth.

Hands gripped her from behind, and baritone bass music echoed through her mind.

—bop, do-wop, bop, bop, bop, bom, bom, bop—

"Did you come back for more? I can always do it again. Again and again."

"Stop it!" she shrieked.

He was going to snap her neck. And she was powerless. His grip was iron. Inevitable.

But she was half expecting it this time. She gripped his hands with hers and deliberately fell forward, pulling him into the pit with her.

The haunting whispers of the sirens shifted into the begging, crying screams of lost spirits. A black ocean drew them into its endless depths.

CHAPTER 12
THE SEA OF SHADOWS

LUKIE WAILED IN THE DARKNESS. She recalled the twenty years she'd spent in the Underworld.

They all sucked.

If she'd been asked to imagine the realm of the dead while a living teenager, she would have thought of beautiful, melancholy scenery, like a Vizzie Slanter music video. Autumnal trees weeping red leaves, empty swings in a park, castle ruins wide open to an empurpled sky with smoke machine fog billowing around the corners of the set.

But Tenebra wasn't like that. It was an ants' nest. Full of trapped dead people obsessing over their lost lives.

And her impression of velvet ocean waters was wrong. The void of Tenebra was *acid*. It burned away the substance of the weaker spirits. No wonder revenants ate souls. That's what Tenebra itself did—it corroded memories slowly until all that was left were disembodied whispers.

There were three ways to survive.

First, build. Ghosts walled themselves into fortresses of their own obsessions and recollections to protect themselves. These structures floated in the void like castles within a fish tank, some only a few rooms wide, others entire cities.

Second, run. Swimming through the devouring ocean, attempting to find safe places to hide on the outskirts of the psyche-fortresses, always moving away from the predators. Losing precious memories but trying to stay safe and sane throughout the years.

And last, hunt. Follow the runners, eat them, and consume their essence. Survive at the cost of becoming a fragmented jigsaw being as your spirit's identity was replaced with a patchwork of recollections.

Lukie had run. She had crawled along the outskirts of the sealed psyche fortresses, desperately moving ahead of the hunters chasing her. She'd slunk through tunnels, hidden in blackened caves, floated into falling pockets trying to keep her own self intact, needing to survive long enough so she didn't lose everything.

But something was different this time. A luminous property surrounded her. Protecting her very essence from being eroded by the surrounding void.

Okay, back in Tenebra. Where's the monster? Where's Cage and the two missing kids?

There was no one with her. But that was the nature of Tenebra. It kept you isolated.

Panic made her churn and spiral within the abyss. She needed to get out of here. Every year she lost was another year that separated her from Dad.

Memories flashed of a familiar place. An old apartment building with peeling paint walls and threadbare carpet. A set of stairs, heading upwards. A concrete floor covered in chalk marks. Something about the location resonated with her. She reached forward—

—and she was *there*.

In a street in a rundown inner-city district. Buildings were jammed up against each other like books, brown-bricked and dusted with soot. The sky above was smoke-gray, cut through with streaks of yellow light like marbled fat.

Lukie was standing at a bus shelter. Faded movie posters were pasted on the walls. Opposite was a five-story-high apartment block, its exterior beaten and scarred like a dockside prize fighter. Illegible chalk marks from childish games marked the concrete pavement in front of it.

Knowing somehow that the building was important, Lukie crossed the road. The chipped blue doors at the entrance banged in the muggy breeze that stirred through the streets. Stairs covered in worn, threadbare carpet headed upwards.

Footsteps echoed on the stairs above.

Someone else was here.

"Hey!" she called out, but the footsteps receded. She *knew* who they belonged to. Someone familiar, like an old friend.

Lukie ran. Up one flight of stairs, then two. The door to the third floor closed shut in her face just as she arrived. She bashed it open, revealing a corridor with yellow cracking plaster walls spotted with mildew.

"It's me!" Lukie tried.

The footsteps vanished around a previously unseen corner. Lights trembled in their sockets.

"Hello?" Lukie called out.

Something glinted at her feet. She picked up a battered toy car—one of those round-hooded ones seen in 1940s movies—just as a nearby door clicked close.

"Wait!" Lukie stopped outside. Overwhelming familiarity flooded her. Playing in this corridor with her cars. Staring out the cracked glass windows over the city unfolding below. Feeling alive as she strode along the rooftops above the smog and oily streetlights.

Lukie held her head. Those weren't her memories. She was sure of it. She'd never, never lived anywhere other than

Breakwater Bay. Swallowing, Lukie thumped on the door. "Listen, I'm lost."

"I've already helped you. Now leave me alone." The voice sounded like a child's, low and whispering.

"You already—" Lukie sank to her knees. She *knew* the apartment on the other side of that door. A tiny kitchen. Three matchbox bedrooms. Everything painted a nice cream because the old man had taken more care of their home than their landlord. A fierce grief for a lost father rose within her, mixed up with the smell of car oil and tobacco.

Those weren't her memories. They had to be from someone else. Her patron, who'd given up part of their own soul to empower Lukie.

Cage had said ghosts strong enough to create revenants were the true lords of Tenebra, powerful and obsessed.

But this ghost was a child hiding in their apartment.

"You sent me back!" Lukie rested her head against the door. Shouldn't her patron be more welcoming? "But I can't remember what we spoke about."

The child sighed. "You wanted to find a girl and sing to her."

"That's it?" Lukie slumped to her knees.

"Pretty much. Something also about finding your father and your friends. I told you things wouldn't be the same, but you didn't listen."

"Karra." Lukie wiped her nose. "I abandoned her at the party. I don't know where she is."

"Red Jack's Help's House."

"Who?"

"Red Jack." Her patron had a faint, superior edge to her tone. The child thought she was *stupid*. "He's a ghost who has a castle of chains and blood. Red Jack made a revenant. Another filthy killer. Now that revenant built a place in Tenebra. He's got guests that have been staying with him for a long time. Your girl's there."

"How do I get to her?" Lukie twisted her hands around.

"You have connections in common. Think of somewhere you know, and if it resonates, it might be one of the rooms in Red Jack's Help's House. It was built by a revenant, so it's not stable. You can get in if you find the right hole."

"When I fought... Red Jack's Help, I wasn't strong enough. He killed me before." Lukie locked her fingers together. "Can you give me more powers?"

"Not now. You have to want something in such a big way that I can channel it to you. Red Jack's Help wanted a place to himself so bad, and then his master gave him the power to make the house. I imagine it'll work the same for you. Remember, you've only got a few hours to sort out your unfinished business."

"What? Why?"

"You were like a cat begging for scraps. You wouldn't go away. I lent a hand. But giving you a vestige *hurt*. So, I'm taking it back at sunrise. Better get moving and find that girl." The footsteps retreated deeper into the apartment, and a door slammed shut from within.

"I'm sorry!" she yelled after a few seconds.

Her patron didn't respond.

A stray cat? That's all I am to her? Lukie had thought that meeting her patron would grant her a greater sense of purpose and comfort. Instead, the mysterious, all-powerful ghost lord was an upset child.

Lukie only had a few hours to finish off what she needed to do. But she couldn't waste time stewing on the fleeting nature of undead existence. *Think of it like a second chance and stay focused on finding Karra.*

Driven by renewed urgency, she trudged outside the apartment building and sat at the bus shelter opposite, watching litter tumble past on a hot, dry wind. She fumbled in her pocket and pulled out her cassette and car keys. Her artifacts glowed with a soft, warm light that made her homesick. She missed her family photograph once more.

She put the cassette away. The keys were the easiest focus to use while trying to get somewhere.

Time to enter Red Jack's Help's House.

CHAPTER 13
RED JACK'S HELP'S HOUSE

LUKIE TRIED DIFFERENT RECOLLECTIONS. Whispers Café, where she and Karra would meet for pancakes and caramel milkshakes. Terek's garage where they practiced. The parking lot of Blitz Burgers.

But nothing resonated across the void of Tenebra until she imagined the school library where they had spent so many lunchtimes talking.

And then she was *there*, in a place that should have been familiar.

She was used to the brown squares of carpet. Rows of metal shelves and plastic-covered books. A rack near the front with the latest recommended teenage reads that the librarian hoped would be picked up. On the oaken walls of the library hall hung the prize shields, where each year the top student in their subject had their name printed in gold letters against the burnished wood.

In one corner was the reading lounge, filled with mismatched bean bags and comfortable reading chairs, claimed by the Spook Club and not contested, as the other students viewed the lounge as not cool. They had spent hours here, talking about music, their breakout hits and tours, the weekend, changing the world, and sometimes homework.

But the details for *this* version of the library weren't right.

The carpet was orange. The shelves were wooden. The rack of reads wasn't there, and the lounge was full of stiff leather chairs rather than bean bags.

She crammed her car keys in her pocket. *Am I in Red Jack's Help's House? Or did I get it wrong?*

Glass chimes cracked against each other. Behind Lukie was an open hole that led to the Tenebran void, and something was crawling through it. It was hominin-shaped, but made of shadow and hunched with long, grasping claws. Its head quivered as it sniffed the air.

A hungry ghost. Jagged soul fragments filled its spectral belly, clanking like broken glass bottles. A babble of disjointed memories bubbled from the shade's distorted form. It had fed recently.

Dying in a white bed, alone.

A new baby! Let's call it Sarrael.

I so want to kill you.

It raised claws into the air. Driven by long ages of running and hiding from these things, Lukie threw herself at the shade, pushing at its amorphous shape, wrestling it back toward the void.

Their substances briefly overlapped. Memories of fear bloomed from the predator.

The shadow stretched out a clawed hand, touching Lukie's arm. It pulled aside, whimpering. Sensing the *something else* within her. The invisible glue holding her together. Her temporary *vestige*.

Help me.

"How?" Lukie scrabbled away from it while keeping it in full sight

Why would I help you? Leave me alone. I don't need you or anyone.

It took Lukie a startled moment to realize what was happening. "Did a ghost say that to you? They refused to give you a vestige?"

The shade reached out with its shadowy fingers. Begging.

Lukie's hands tensed.

She had been hunted by these monsters for twenty years. Who knew how much of her past she'd lost to their claws? Why show pity to something that would have gleefully eaten her if she didn't have a vestige? On the other hand, she'd been like this creature once.

Tamlyn had stopped her from going crazy by feeding her one of his memories. Now to see if that worked on shades as well as revenants. Lukie selected an unimportant event—a high school lunch hour, sitting with her friends—and visualized the scene as a photograph in her hand.

She held a bundle of sensations. The itchiness of her uniform, the smell of the homemade perfume that Karra had given her, rendered from crushed roses taken from her mother's garden. The warmth of morning sunlight. Chatter about random stuff—about the weekend, and when their band would tour the world.

The shade snatched the photograph and ate it. The memory died within Lukie like a candle snuffing out, and a pain stabbed her deep inside.

I shouldn't have done that. So stupid. No wonder my patron wants her vestige back.

The shade lingered.

"You can go now," Lukie ordered. "Return to the void."

The shade burped. *I can't wait until school's out.* It padded toward her expectantly, like a stray cat. Lukie had fed it a memory of her high school friendship—warm, summer, drifting days—and it believed it belonged with her via the false experience.

"Stay here," Lukie ordered, not wanting the monster to be with her in case it attacked. "I've got to find Karra."

Time to explore the library. Why was it so *orange*?

She went to the music section and grabbed a book at random. The words were a blur. The person who made this memory hadn't read the text.

She put the book back. Next stop: the library's front counter. As Lukie passed the polished wooden trophy shields, she craned her head, attempting to see her own name against the class of 1983 music prize, but the last year on the board was 1963.

There was something different about the athletics prize shield. The wood glowed with a buttery light, and the last year had a name written in metallic ink:

1963. Baron Shark.

"Who?" That couldn't be real. She wondered what the actual version of the shield said. The soft resonance reminded her of when she'd handled her artifacts earlier. She pulled out her keys, compared their similar golden aura to the shield, and put them away.

No wonder this version of the library was awful—they hadn't understood color coordination in the 1960s. Lukie flung the door wide and stopped.

Outside should have been a concrete ramp that led to the school quad, covered in gravel and encircled by the science block and language laboratory. Instead, it opened into a messy room, with an unmade bed, an acoustic guitar on the floor, and discarded t-shirts. Posters of popular 1960s bands hung on the wall. The Pineapple Dapples. Beach-au-Bomb. Lukie winced at the teenage boy funk emanating from the room. *It's not that hard to wash your sheets. And you need to put your instruments away in their cases when you finish with them. Loser.*

Her patron had said that Red Jack's Help's House wasn't stable. It was memory rooms leading into each other without any sensible connections like roads or corridors. *But memories aren't concerned with that. You just think of the places you want most, rather than how you got there.*

Isn't Mrs. Barker hot? The shade asked behind her.

"Stop following me!" Lukie snapped at it. It was one thing to help it, another to have it constantly trail her. And this must be how her patron thought of her.

She closed the door and opened it again without thinking of any location. This time it revealed the void. Cold wind blew on her face, and she heard the distant susurrations of a thousand voices whispering at once. Lukie slammed it shut and leaned against it, breathing heavily. *A hole. It's a wonder this place isn't crawling with shades.*

"I have to find Karra," Lukie said.

My favorite gum is the blue one, burbled the shade behind her.

She closed her eyes. A memory of school had gotten her here, but she didn't want to spend a long time wandering through Red Jack's Help's inconsequential recollections.

She held her keys and thought of the beach house. The site of the party, and where she'd died, and the sensation of Karra's lips against hers.

A warm sense filled her. A connection.

She opened the door again.

It led outside into the evening. Golden sunlight washed behind a wall of shadowy pine trees. Over to the east, the sky darkened above the ocean. And the beach house stood on top of the cliff as it had done in her time.

CHAPTER 14
THE REUNION

FOR A FEW BRIEF SECONDS, Lukie hoped that she'd found her magic portal back to 1983. But things weren't right. The beach house was surrounded by twenty or so big cars with ornamental hoods and fins. And the party music was slower than what she was used to: full of rhythms and harmonies. Currently playing: 'You Sparkle Larkle Me' by the Pineapple Dapples, one of Dad's favorites. A hit in 1963.

Can I borrow your pencils for art class? I left mine at home.

Lukie folded her arms and glared at the shade which had followed her. "My pencils are in the trees way over there."

The shade burbled and scampered off in the direction she pointed. Sighing with relief, Lukie walked toward the house.

"Hey!" another voice said. "80s elf girl!" A woman ran up to her, waving her hands. "It's me, Maz! Sorry for running you over. I keep telling Ger he needs to pay more attention to the road when he talks about football! Glad to see you're okay!"

"It's Lukie. And are you all right?"

"Why wouldn't I be?" Maz shook her head.

As far as Lukie knew, Cage, Maz, and her boyfriend had

been thrown into Tenebra. Were they alive, and could they get out of here? Or were they dead?

Maz tapped her feet against the ground. "Well, maybe not. This will sound crazy, but I don't have a clue where we are. This can't be the same house. And we weren't going to a 1960s party. I would have worn something completely different." Her eyes grew wide. "Wait! Ger? Where is he? He was right here…" Her hands flailed at the empty space by her side. She rubbed at her face. "We were just in the pine forest having some fun. I don't know what happened after that."

Deciding not to tell the woman that she *might* be dead—after all, Lukie wasn't completely certain how this place worked—Lukie shook her head. "I'm not sure what's going on either. It's been a wild night. Did you see a man with silver hair?"

Cage would be handy right now.

"No. I better not be tripping. I've been trying to get off glaze and stick to beer. Did you do anything before?"

Lukie remembered teenage Nathel handing her an open can of Thunder Cola. "Wait. Did you talk to an older guy this evening? Blond hair, may have gone on about poetry. He wore an Outside Sky t-shirt."

"Oh yeah." Maz squinted up at the moon, thinking. "Him. Outside Sky—that's an old band. Didn't the lead singer die of a drug overdose in the 80s?"

"What? No, that's completely wrong." *Or is it? Why didn't I ask Tam about Vizzie? No, no.* She pushed that knot of pain away for later. "Did the dark poetry guy give you a drink?"

"Yeah, some beers," Maz admitted. "He was really friendly. Wanted Gerron and I to have a good time."

Lukie clenched her fists. Nathel spiking drinks. *How come no one's caught him by now? Is he the monster?*

"Well, let's see if our boys are at the party." Maz walked toward the house.

Lukie trailed after her. As soon as they opened the door, a man with horn-rimmed glasses peered out, saying, "New people!"

Couples danced, twisting and spinning around on the floor. Some clung to the edges, talking in small groups, and holding drinks. All of them were human. No full or blended other types of hominins were in sight. Men were dressed in tight collared white shirts and black ties; women wore boots, red or cream blouses, and matching skirts. The band played on the corner, their lyrics filled with do-wops and ma-ba-ma-ra fragments.

"Welcome!" a voice called out. A woman regally descended the spiral staircase.

Lukie froze.

It was *Karra*. Not dressed like she usually did with a long black dress and silver jewelry. Her dark kinky hair was braided back into dozens of tiny braids that were twisted onto her head in an elaborate bun. She wore a white miniskirt, thigh-high matching leather boots, and a lace-collared shirt.

"You're alive!" Lukie gasped, forgetting briefly that she was in the Underworld.

"No," Karra said crisply.

Heart racing, Lukie reached out to envelop Karra in a crushing embrace. But Karra strode past, focusing on Maz. "You need to be made presentable. This way." She looped an arm around the other woman and pulled her toward the staircase.

"Have you seen my man, Gerron?" Maz asked. "Big guy."

"Is he full human?" Karra asked.

"Half-ogre on his mother's side," Maz said. "He's really funny and sweet. He just got a football scholarship to Port Bloodsand Uni."

"I'm afraid he won't be here." Karra tugged her upstairs.

Lukie trailed after them, shut-out and bewildered.

"Is there another party where Ger is?" Maz asked. "Sorry, I'm so confused right now. Must have had some glaze."

"You wouldn't want to be where he is," Karra said. "Let's just get you changed, and you'll soon pick up on how this place works."

Maz clamped her jaw shut and let Karra guide her up the stairs.

Lukie followed them into a large bedroom stuffed full of 1960s clothing on wardrobe racks. She'd seen enough old movies with Dad to understand there'd been a huge variety of fashions from that era: long paisley skirts, bell bottom jeans, leather jackets.

But that wasn't here. Instead, there were only rows of miniskirts and blouses for the women, and white shirts, black trousers for men.

Karra selected a crimson miniskirt from a rack.

"I hate short skirts," Maz said. "Do you have any of those cool yellow sundresses?"

"No," Karra said. "It's what he likes."

"Who?" Lukie interrupted. She leaned against the door frame, fingers digging into the wall.

"The Baron," Karra said. "This is his house."

"Are you okay?"

"It could be worse. You've seen the hungry ones outside. You need to go."

"Why?"

Why isn't she happy to see me? We've just found each other again.

"He doesn't like half-breeds." Karra's voice was distant. "This is a bad place for you to be. Find somewhere else to hide."

"But—"

"I need to help this girl, otherwise any pain she suffers will be your fault." Karra focused on fixing Maz's hair.

"I'm in danger?" Maz tried to stand up, but Karra forced her into the seat.

Half-breed? Karra had never called her that before.

Lukie had arrived in this place determined to find and save Karra. But Karra didn't want to be helped. Hadn't even been glad to see Lukie.

I thought we'd run away together and it would all be fine.

Her eyes stung, but she went downstairs and rejoined the party.

The white-tiled floor of the beach house was as she remembered. The great doors were open, letting in the evening ocean breeze. A band played at the far corner of the plaza, and couples danced and twisted in rhythmic clockwork. A trestle table was covered in red plastic cups and bottles of booze.

I'll just give Karra some space. Then I'll try again to save her. Is this place a prison? I should talk to some of these people.

Walking over to the drink table, Lukie cleared her throat and addressed a man watching the crowd with a blank expression on his face. "Hey, what's happening here?"

"Well, the band's playing Tra-la-la Trail and a pretty girl is looking at me. Want to dance?"

"Sure." Lukie grabbed his arm. Music trickled past. A few beats and missed notes. Something was wrong—his soul had been eaten. He was barely self-aware. All he really knew about himself was that he was at a party and would have a good time. A few facts about school and the weather lingered in his mind, enough so he could hold a general conversation, but that was it. He'd gone from being the star of his own life to a nameless extra.

Lukie excused herself and quickly brushed up against two more partygoers—a man in a plaid jacket, and a woman with cat's eye spectacles—while trying not to feel creepy. Their soul music was barely holding together—a few erratic beats or monotones, like someone holding down the same note on a synthesizer.

She approached a man with slicked-back hair who looked more alert.

"Hey!"

"Get away from me." He pushed her and retreated. A skittering of nervous piano music danced through her mind. "You stand out too much."

"I'm here to help."

"Do it somewhere else." The man collected the blank-eyed woman in the cat's eye spectacles and dragged her to the dance floor.

Eventually, Karra and Maz arrived. The girl from 2003 had her hair piled high, and she wore a red miniskirt, white pullover, and blouse. Like every other woman at the party.

Lukie approached again. "Hey."

"I want to get out of here." Maz sniffed.

"One day," Karra said. "Until then, we dress to fit in."

"You kept your memories. A lot of people here haven't," Lukie said.

"Because I chose to survive," Karra said.

"How do I defeat him?" Lukie persisted. That was what she was here to do. Stop Red Jack's Help. Get everyone to safety. "Does he have a secret weakness?"

"This isn't an adventure game," Karra snapped back.

"There must be something!"

"He likes to win," Karra admitted.

"We should go—"
"He's here!" the doorman called.
Lukie hid in the crowd just as the Baron entered.

CHAPTER 15
BARON SHARK

LUKIE HAD BEEN EXPECTING ROYALTY. Flowing locks, ermine-trimmed cloak, even a suit of shining armor. But this man had sun-bronzed skin, a faded tank-top that read 'Baron Shark 1963!' and shoulder-length, tousled, metallic golden hair.

The Baron was a surfer dude.

And he strongly resembled Nathel.

A spurt of manic energy rippled across the gathering. Like a light switch had been suddenly flicked on, people waved, cheered, and toasted the Baron's presence.

"Everyone enjoying the festivities?" the Baron called out. Nathel's voice, but not quite.

The crowd applauded and raised glasses.

This is such bullshit! Can't he see they're all faking it?

The band played a song with a faster tempo, and the dancing couples pulled back in stage-like unison as Karra presented Maz to the Baron.

"Why, the new girl I saved." The Baron ran his fingers down the side of Maz's face. "Welcome to my domain of Clearwater."

"Thanks, but I really need to find my man Gerron!" Maz said. "He's tall, an ogre on his mother's side—"

Karra glared furiously, suggesting that Maz was disobeying a prior briefing about behavior.

The Baron chuckled. He gripped Maz with big, clenching hands.

A chill stabbed through Lukie. Even though she'd only seen him before as a shadowy figure, she knew that laugh. And those hands.

It was the monster that had killed her. The Baron twisted Maz's arm in a lock and forced her to her knees. "Are you suggesting I'd fraternize with a half-breed *ogre?*"

"Stop it!" Maz cried. "You're hurting me!"

His free hand gripped the side of Maz's neck.

Some of the crowd inched back, others watched with blank smiles.

The Baron fed on Maz. Her soul-music—a funky, brassy dance beat—faded as it slid down the Baron's gullet.

Oh shit, she'll end up a mind-zombie like a lot of the people here if he doesn't stop soon. No one is doing anything. They're too scared. I can't do anything… But I promised Tam I'd try.

Give me the power to destroy him! She thought at her patron, desperately hoping for a blast of searing energy to crisp the Baron to ashes.

Nothing happened.

And Maz was still being fed on.

"Stop that!" Lukie ran forward, her fear of the Baron nearly overwhelming her. All she could think of was the world's stupidest plan.

"*You.* Back for *more?*" He released his hands, flexing them.

"I'm here to challenge you." Her words sounded so foolish.

"And how do you propose to do that?" The Baron folded his arms. "Go on. Tell me."

Lukie tried again to summon a burst of Baron-burning power, but nothing happened. Stupid patron.

Back to the plan.

"A contest. If you're up for it."

His eyes widened with interest, and he leaned forward. "And the stakes?"

"If I win, everyone gets to leave your party."

"Very well. I feel we could use some entertainment this evening. I will release my retainers if you win our contest. And what sort of little competition did you have in mind? I imagine it's something that you've got a chance at. Skipping? Marbles? Folding paper dolls?" His smile was so smug that Lukie wanted to punch him right there.

Lukie pointed at the bandstand in the corner. "A singing contest!"

"Very well. I'm feeling magnanimous this evening." The Baron gestured at Karra. "My bride, and our gracious hostess, will be the judge."

Karra fiddled with a golden ring on her finger. It replaced the silver skull ring that Lukie had given her once.

Bride? Lukie wailed. How had she not noticed that ring before? *What does he mean by bride?*

The Baron stretched languidly, walked up to the bandstand.

The man holding the microphone handed it to the Baron and scurried off stage. The Baron gestured at the band and played 'Summertime' by the Beach-au-Bombs, singing:

> "Now my home turf is a great place to surf
> But once a year you gotta stay clear
> Because the world's biggest wave comes to drag
>   you to your grave
> So they close off the beach and the water's out
>   of reach

"We go down to the park and wait for Baron
    Shark
And he says 'Come and see, no one can ride that
    wave but me'
He walks down the water and prepares for the
    slaughter
He's got a golden board that cuts the waves like
    a sword."

Lukie was sure that 'Baron Shark' didn't appear in the original version of the song. But she had to admit he could perform well with a slick, professional baritone, singing about a reckless surfer that risked his life on the biggest wave of the year.

When the Baron finished, he bowed deeply. The room was filled with cheers and applause. Karra clapped loudly, face flushed with joy.

The Baron beckoned Lukie to the stage.

She gripped the microphone. The Baron held it for a second longer than he had to, his cool blue gaze regarding her, his lips quirked into a habitual smirk.

Lukie tugged the mic free, and the Baron sauntered from the stage.

She didn't know many 1960s songs, so she borrowed a guitar from a band member and clipped the microphone into the stand. She stared out into the blank-faced crowd.

Am I really trying to defeat the guy who murdered me with a singing contest? This must be the stupidest idea in the world. But it's not like I can just rip him apart.

The soul-eaten people smiled and clapped, but a few of the more alert party prisoners watched with secret hope.

Karra was watching, her face blank.

Lukie took a deep breath. Hands sweating. What she needed to do was to reach Karra.

Lukie strummed the opening chords to Invisible Youth, the most 80s song she knew. Something that she and Spook Club had practiced late in the afternoons in her garage.

> "I see you in the busy street
> Flesh, cars, concrete
> One day you'll wake up
> One day you'll shake up."

As she sang, she concentrated solely on Karra. Trying to will her free from the Baron's control. Reminding her of ice creams after school, passing notes in class, kissing under the old tree in Maple Park.

Karra was listening. Her icy exterior cracked—a single wet tear dripped down her cheek.

I did it! I got through to her. Now she'll leave with me.

The 80s guitar crescendo hung in the air. Its rawness disrupted the crisp, uniform edge of the Baron's party. A few people mouthed the chorus along with her; more were trapped out of their time.

Lukie finished. Her heart raced and sweat dripped from her. She'd never felt so alive after a song. For a few brief seconds, she really believed that she won, and that the Baron would honor the terms of the contest.

But then he smiled, displaying white even teeth, and Lukie's stomach curdled with fear.

"I see you liked her song more," the Baron told Karra. "No need to hide it. But I'm feeling magnanimous this evening." He waved a hand around the room. "You can all leave freely —into the howling void outside."

CHAPTER 16
THE CHASE

"THAT'S RIGHT," the Baron said. He gestured at Lukie. "Tonight's *comedy routine* was a little reminder for you all. Outside, there is only darkness. The shades will come for you, suck your memories dry, make you as they are." His voice dropped to a reasonable tone. "Now compare that to what I offer here. A safe existence. My reign is just, my lands offer you warmth and safety."

"Where is this place?" Maz croaked.

The Baron crouched by her side. "Why didn't she tell you?" He pointed at Lukie. "This is the Underworld. You're dead, my dear. The realm of hungry ghosts. And I alone saved you." He whispered loudly in her ear. "Remember the screams, the falling void, the voices over and over again."

"Stop it, stop it!" Maz snapped, placing her hands over her ears.

"Remember," the Baron commanded, "oblivion awaits you outside. Be grateful for what I have given you." He toed her with a boot.

"Karra, come with me!" Lukie pointed at the door and held out her hand.

"Go on, my dear," the Baron said. "Follow your little mongrel friend back into the abyss."

"There's a place I can take you," Lukie begged, thinking of her patron's memory palace.

"Is it like this?" Karra hissed. "A cage?"

"Well…" Lukie thought of the lonely apartment block, the peeling wallpaper. The loneliness of the child ghost. And then she lost Karra with that hesitation.

"I'm not going with you."

"But…"

"What's the point? You can't protect me. You can't get me out of here. You can't defeat him!" Karra pointed at the Baron who was studying his fingernails. "He only let you win because it amused him. Why are you here at all?"

"To save you! From him! After he killed—"

"You had your chance!" Karra screamed. "We could have gotten away from the party that night. Even gone to Storm City. Another would have been chosen. But *no*, it had to all be about *you*. You had to sing, you had to perform. The band should have broken up months earlier. We only stuck together because of your incessant whining! I kept telling you how the boys were harassing me, and you wouldn't listen. You self-absorbed bitch! It was always about you! Your music, your future, and never about anyone else. Well, I'm through with you! If this is all I get, so be it!" She finished her tirade, spittle smearing her perfect lipstick.

She hates me. Was I that bad? I forced everyone to stay together. Why did no one say anything to me?

"Your makeup is smeared." The Baron pointed to Karra's face. "Take the new girl upstairs. Return when you're presentable."

Karra quietly pulled Maz to her feet, and the two of them retreated up the spiral staircase.

Lukie trudged to the door. She had no idea what to do

now. All her dreams, hopes—they'd all been shattered. Time to get out of here.

"Wait." The Baron's cold voice cut into her consciousness. "I said if you 'won' the contest, *they* could leave. Not you."

A memory of panic flared within Lukie. Running along the beach. Heavy footsteps pounding on the sand after her.

It was going to happen again.

Lukie ran outside. She tried a nearby car, but it was locked.

The Baron followed her out of the house. His eyes glinted a luminous blue in the evening light. A few of the partygoers flanked him like courtiers.

No, no, no.

She sprinted into the pines, breath wheezing. She stumbled over twisted pieces of driftwood and nearly jarred her leg in a hole.

Footsteps thumped behind her.

She broke through the tree line. The cliff's edge loomed in front of her. The sea boomed and hissed against the rocks below, and a bloody sunset stained the sky.

This isn't right! I was heading away from the cliff! I shouldn't be here!

The shadowy shape of the Baron cut through the trees.

There was nowhere else to go. She ran along the cliff and down the stairs to the beach. Her breath wheezed. Steady footsteps indicated that the Baron was close behind her.

Lukie fled across the sand. In the distance, the Pillars of Majesty loomed like blood-coated spears in the red sunset. Her lungs nearly exploded, and her palms dripped sweat.

Without warning, he was on top of her, gripping her, pushing her down onto the sand. A cacophony of bass singing raged through her mind.

—ba-mar-ma-ra, bop-she-bop, do-wop, bom, bom, bop—

"Let go of me!" she croaked. She fumbled for his soul

music, trying to drink it, but it overwhelmed her like a raging wave.

"You're going to tell me about the hunter!" The Baron dragged her from the beach to the tide line. She kicked impotently at the sand, failing to push his hands away from her. Spots danced in front of her eyes.

The sound of swirling water intensified.

"What is he?" the Baron demanded. "Are there more of him? My king wants to know."

"I'm not telling you anything!" Lukie rasped.

"Pathetic. This time I'll devour every last scrap of you. Your secrets will be mine."

I need power! Help me destroy him! she screamed to her patron.

I need a green pencil for my homework tonight. It was the shade, appearing next to her, its head tilted to one side in confusion.

"Help!" she begged.

The shade had every right to abandon her. She'd pushed it away. Mocked it. It was drunk on a memory of false friendship.

But it lunged and cut the Baron with its knife-sharp claws. Oily smoke boiled out of his wound. He stepped back and then punched his hand into the shadow. Little sparks of its substance—her donated memories—flared off it.

Lukie staggered to her feet, barely able to stand.

Rather than defending itself, the shade slashed the air open behind it. The vision of the sky and sea tore away like a play's backdrop, revealing the Tenebran void.

Lukie leaped into the hole. "Follow me!" she screamed at the shade.

But all she could see was the Baron staring at her with his luminous blue eyes, wiping the shade's essence from his lips.

CHAPTER 17
THE MONSTER

2:00AM, 8 BLOODSTONE 2003

SHE WAS LYING on the beach, midnight water lapping her frozen ankles.

This was where she died and had crawled out of Tenebra, borne by her obsession to reclaim her old life. To see Dad again, to change the world with her music, to find her friends once more.

But she'd failed. Dad was gone. Her insistence at performing at the 1983 party had led to Karra's death. Worse, her princess-level demands to keep the band together during their final year of high school had severely strained the bonds of friendship between the group. Nothing was completely clear—the long years in Tenebra had damaged her memory. But there were enough fragments bubbling up in her subconsciousness. Terek wanting to give up Spook Club for football while she threw a tantrum until he stayed. Karra sobbing on her shoulder about something the boys had said, and Lukie saying that they hadn't meant anything bad. Sera asking to play board games and being rebuffed as they had to practice. Nathel showing her his own lyrics, and her crumpling the paper into a ball on the floor, telling him they were rubbish.

Even with the group descending into mutual hatred,

Lukie had a final demand for them. One last concert at the end-of-year party, and they would go their separate ways.

She had been a terrible friend—hadn't listened, trapped them in the band when they should have broken up months earlier.

She was a completely selfish bitch who deserved to be a shitty, undead thing.

A monster.

Cage had been right.

And she wasn't even an effective monster. She hadn't defeated the Baron or rescued Karra. She had been unable to draw on her patron's power. She'd only escaped because the shade, drunk on her high school delusions, had *believed* in the false memories of friendship she'd fed it. The shade had saved her and been devoured for that.

"I'm sorry," she mouthed to the shade. To Karra. To Terek, Nathel, and Tamlyn. To Dad, who she would never see again.

It had all been for nothing.

I'll just sit here and wait for the sunrise to crisp me to ashes. My patron will get her stupid vestige back. I don't care anymore.

"Lukie!" Tamlyn's voice, accompanied by a flashlight, cut through her misery. The detective was coming down the stairs, puffing heavily. "Are you all right? Did you find Cage?"

She shook her head. "I failed. The Baron's got Karra. She hates and blames me—"

"Whoa! Slow down. What happened? Where's Karra?" He tucked his hands under his coat. "Let's get back to my car. I'm freezing."

Lukie told him about Tenebra as they trudged along the beach. About her patron and the Baron. Her failure to use her powers leading to the joke singing contest and her revelation that she was just like one of the monsters that Cage hunted.

As they walked to the car, she saw that the partygoers had

mostly left the ruins. Only a few people remained being questioned by uniformed officers. Two marked police cars were parked in the driveway, blue and red lights flashing.

"It sounds like Cage might still be alive, at least for a bit longer," Tamlyn mused, stroking his stubble. "I'll need your help to—"

"Weren't you listening to me?" Lukie made fists. "I shouldn't be doing anything. I'm a *monster*! I'm responsible for Karra's death."

"You're not the monster. The Baron is." Tamlyn placed a hand on her shoulder.

"But I forced everyone to stay in the band! If it wasn't for me—"

"It was *high school*. It was easier to pretend to be a rock star than to study for exams or face our actual problems. Sure, you were a complete princess, but that doesn't make you the same as a serial killer."

"I should have believed Karra when she said the boys were harassing her."

"Yes, but you can't change that now. None of us communicated well." Tamlyn went over to his car and popped the trunk open, pulling out a bright yellow towel. "I should have done something, but I didn't. Had to be the stupid, silent one."

Lukie held the towel. "I don't need this. I'm an undead *thing*. I can't catch a cold."

"I don't want sand in my car," Tamlyn explained. "Takes ages to vacuum out."

"Oh." Lukie did her best to dust the sand from her soaked clothes. "If only I hadn't been so selfish."

"Everyone was selfish at that age. And you're still a teen, let's face it."

"But—"

"Listen to me." Tamlyn's voice was low and earnest. "Both

of you were killed by this Baron. He ended your lives and messed up your afterlives. Now, are you going to help me take down this bastard or what?"

She didn't want to. The Baron would eat her senseless. Karra would scorn her again. But her old friend was asking for her support and doing *something* beat sitting on the beach waiting to die at sunrise.

"What is your plan?"

"I've got Nathel in custody," Tamlyn explained. "I found him running down the road back to his house, suspicious as hell. But I don't have hard evidence. Which means he'll be released tomorrow when the Clearwater lawyer gets out of bed."

"Do you think he is the Baron?"

"An accomplice," Tamlyn said. "What other family would have a 'Baron' in their midst? Before we go, think hard. Is there anything else that might help us?"

Now that she wasn't wallowing in her own misery, Lukie thought of Tenebra and what she'd seen there.

"I think so. We need to visit the school library."

———

Lukie thought she'd never return to Breakwater Bay High. Maybe years later, when she was a great singer touring for a documentary on her early life, but not tonight. The school was a small series of concrete buildings in a wire fence with a brown grass sports ground outside. A new school hall replaced the old one, but the core of the place she remembered was intact.

Memories of all the times she'd spent here were tainted by her recent recollections about what she'd done to her friends. Tamlyn had hand-waved the events, but he'd had twenty years to process.

Tamlyn pulled up outside the school and parked. "Hey, my sunglasses are in the glove box. No offence, but I don't want you creeping out the janitor."

Lukie opened the glove box, pawed past the collection of country music CDs, and found a set of nice black aviator sunglasses with leather side shields. She wasn't sure where she'd lost her original daisy pair. She slipped them on and checked her appearance in the mirror, fancying she looked like a secret agent.

"You can see in the dark," Tamlyn said.

"What? It's like early evening." Lukie peered outside.

"The streetlights are out in this section," Tamlyn said. "Can you read out some of my CD titles?"

She dug through his collection of CDs. "'My Home on the Ranch,' 'This Country Coast', 'The Elf with the Golden Guitar'—you really have lost all taste."

Tamlyn snorted laughter, and they left the car.

Peppan, the school janitor, now bald and stout compared to how he'd been in 1983, emerged from a battered utility truck. He wore shorts and a faded t-shirt.

"Thanks for meeting me here so late," Tamlyn said.

"No worries." Peppan squinted at Lukie, frowned, and shook his head. "Right. School library, you said. Let's get this over with."

The old man grunted. He guided them into the school with a steel flashlight heavy enough to poleaxe a cow.

Lukie trudged behind them, feeling the difference of twenty years. That fishpond where they'd sat at morning tea was now replaced by a sculpture. Huge trees rose out of the gardens that she remembered being seedlings planted on Nature Day. The old gravel quad was paved over, and posters advertised new school plays and festivals she hadn't heard of.

One night for her. Twenty years for the world. Even with magic, she wasn't able to revisit 1983 to save everyone.

She'd have to atone for her crimes in the here and now.

Peppan limped up the concrete ramp, favoring his left knee. At the top, he entered a code into an alarm panel and unlocked the school library door, flashing his light along the rows of wooden prize shields on the entrance wall.

Her name was still there—*Lukenaria Carpenter*—winner of the 1983 music award. Other names came after her, some she recognized and some she didn't. What had happened to those musicians? Had they joined famous bands? Played at pubs, or got into the kingdom's Top Ten?

"There," Tamlyn pointed up at the athletics shield. "Is it what you think it is?"

Lukie read the entry for 1963. "Brandas Clearwater. That must be him."

"I remember." Peppan lit a cigarette. "He won all the local surfing competitions. He died in a car accident. Just after graduating. Ran off the road and smashed into the Pillars of Majesty."

"Do you recall anything else?" Tamlyn asked.

Peppan squinted. "Bit of an arrogant boor, like most of the Clearwaters. Had it in for half-breeds and non-humans. Still carrying a chip about the lost barony. Got suspended for beating up a dwarrow-mix once." He glanced at Lukie, side-long. "That's about it. Might be some more information in the local papers if the town library hadn't burned down."

The shield had glowed with a particular resonance when she'd viewed it from the Baron's memory shack, but would it really be one of his artifacts?

"Can you get it down?" Lukie asked.

Peppan tucked his cigarette behind his left ear—a habit that had always unnerved Lukie—puffed and pulled and unhooked the award shield, and then handed it over.

The chill from it cut into her undead fingers. It was a thing of Tenebra. What sort of arrogant jerk would leave their artifact hanging up for all to see?

Him.

"This is it."

"We'll need to borrow it for a while," Tamlyn said.

"Why?" Peppan asked.

"This might help us find out what happened to those girls in '83."

The janitor reclaimed his cigarette. "Wouldn't surprise me if it was a Clearwater. Like a clan of cockroaches, they are."

CHAPTER 18

THE INTERVIEW
3:32AM, 8 BLOODSTONE 2003

THE POLICE INTERVIEW room was a small concrete box. Lukie had thought they were supposed to have a wall of two-way glass, but Tamlyn had laughed when she had mentioned it. A dingy domed light illuminated the stained walls, its innards marked with the shadows of dead moths. Lukie waited outside the door, peering in.

Nathel folded his arms, leaning back on a small plastic chair. Even with his face lined, he was nevertheless the arrogant poet prankster that Lukie remembered. "Hello, Sera. I'm not saying anything. You can hold me for six hours, then what? You'll still have nothing."

"Want a drink?" Tamlyn didn't react to the use of his previous name. Instead, he took a deep draught from his huge coffee mug. He sat with his back to Lukie, facing Nathel across a small table. "A sandwich?"

"Stop it with this good cop bullshit. I'm not telling you anything."

"Three people went missing tonight. You can help."

"I don't know what you're talking about." Nathel stared at the ceiling.

Tamlyn pulled a photograph from his pocket and placed it

directly in front of Nathel. "Let's start with the couple. The woman is Maz Hunter. She's studying nursing. The man is Gerron Axebridge. He's going to Port Bloodsand University next year on a football scholarship. Two young people. Do you know they were engaged? They have their entire futures ahead of them."

Nathel kept looking upwards.

"Just like us once, eh? When we finished school, we were ready to seize the world."

"I'm not telling you anything," Nathel cut in. "You've no evidence. I'll see that you lose your job over this."

"Some witnesses said they saw you giving away free beers at the old beach house. Gerron had five, according to the statement."

"Nothing illegal. It's good to encourage the tourists. They are the only thing keeping this town afloat."

"You pointed Maz and Gerron toward the pine forest near the ruins. You were reported saying 'I'll show you the best spot for it.' What did you mean by that?"

"Just showing them around. Local color, and all that."

"That was the last sighting of them. Going into the woods. We found some blood in a clearing. Signs of a struggle. Are they still alive?"

"I don't know what you're talking about. I'm not responsible for what happens to stupid tourists."

"Your partner is."

"I don't have a partner."

"You must know him. I hear he's—supernatural."

"You're insane." Nathel crossed his arms. "Supernatural? What do you take me for?"

Tamlyn knocked on the desk. Lukie let herself into the interrogation room and closed the door behind her. She walked in front of Nathel and pulled off her sunglasses with a dramatic flourish, revealing red, black-speckled eyes.

Nathel scrambled out of his chair, backed against the wall, and thrust his hands into his pockets, visibly trembling.

"Hello, Nathel," Lukie said. "Haven't seen you since—well, a couple of hours, but before that, not until you gave me that spiked drink. Please tell us about the Baron."

Tamlyn had told her to be polite. Remind him of how they used to be friends. But right now, she wanted to crush his throat.

Nathel straightened up, dropping the pretense of ignorance. Sweat gleamed on his face. "I thought… hoped you were just a tourist when I saw you before. A bad memory. But you're just like him."

"No, I'm not, or not completely. But I need your assistance to rescue the victims he took tonight. And to stop him, for good." Lukie stopped moving toward Nathel. She raised her palms to show that she meant no harm.

"You?" Nathel laughed, a trace of hysteria in his voice. "Princess Lukie? So what if you're a revenant? You're still a teenage girl! He's a predator! He's been doing this for thirty years and he can't die."

"That's interesting," Tamlyn interrupted, sipping more coffee. "Quite a few missing persons cases in the area, going back that time. But I'm interested in why a supernatural monster needs an accomplice to drug his targets for them." He drummed his fingers on the table. "If he's that powerful, why does he need you?"

"Brandas Clearwater dragged his left leg when we fought in the clearing," Lukie recalled. "It must have been an injury from when he died in that car crash. He's slow." She wondered why Brandas's undead form was injured. Perhaps she was lucky that her voice and eternal bruise marks were the only scars she had from death. *But still, I'd prefer a limp if I could just sing properly again…*

"Hmm." Tamlyn drank more coffee. "Sounds like you

could have put some distance between you. Why did you stay around, Nathel? Why didn't you run away? I would have. Would you, Lukie?"

"Absolutely," Lukie said. "I would have gone to Storm City."

Nathel gritted his teeth. He rubbed at his sweating face.

"The Clearwater family hasn't left their mansion in years," Tamlyn said. "You're the only one people see. I hope that your sister Eryn's all right. And little Tayn. Or are you and Brandas the only ones rattling around in that old place of yours?"

"They're alive—" Nathel cut his words short.

Tamlyn sipped at his coffee again. "It would be nice if you didn't have to worry about Brandas. Your family could go outside. You wouldn't have to be an accomplice."

"You can't stop him!" Nathel broke like a twig. He hunched his shoulders and buried his face in his hands, a shadow of the person that Lukie remembered.

Lukie folded her arms. "Wait. What if I knew where one of his artifacts was? The special items that empower him."

Nathel looked up at her with red eyes. "What do you take me for? Do you think he'd just leave it lying around?"

"Well, he did." Lukie picked up the shopping bag by her side, bulging with the meter-high athletics prize shield. "He had it hanging at the school."

Nathel touched it and jerked his hand back. "If he senses that you've got it…"

"Then you'd better hurry and help us, yeah?" Tamlyn cleared his throat.

"We will use this to stop him." Lukie hefting the shield, even though she wasn't sure how you turned a revenant's own artefacts against them.

Nathel wiped his nose on his wrist. "I suppose I can tell you a few things."

"Who is he, exactly?" Lukie asked.

"My uncle. He died in a car accident, and then he returned ten years later. Dragging his foot, looking like raw meat. My grandmother was so happy at the time, but then he started to kill people. Brought them back to play." He wiped his nose. "Used to go on about being the Baron. That this was his land, his hunting grounds, and it was our job to serve him. My father was his first retainer. Doing whatever. After Dad, it was my older sister. Until she stopped talking one day. Now it's my burden."

"And no Clearwater tried to stop him?" Tamlyn asked.

"He can't die! He comes back. Dad blew him into chunks of meat and smoke with a hunting rifle in the day when he's weak. We celebrated, but he returned in the evening. There's no point. And I can't leave, because all the people I care about are hostages. My sister, mother, and little brother. And Terek. If I step out of line, they go."

"And no one's worked out he's been killing for thirty years?"

"There are lots of backpackers. Tourists. Easy to take."

"Why Karra and me?" It was the question Lukie wanted to ask most, even though she knew the answer.

"I hated you so much at the end of high school. You and Karra were going to escape, and I was trapped here with him." He raised his hands. "I kept telling Terek that Karra had the hots for him and a billion other things to make the band a living hell. I'm sorry. I wasn't thinking straight."

Lukie clenched her teeth together. Even though she despised Nathel intensely in this moment, it resonated with the self-loathing inside of her. If she'd treated her friends better, Nathel could have protected them from the Baron. She and Karra would have had a life. But someone else would have died…

"Those kids he took. And Cage. He threw them into a hole. Does that mean they're dead?" Tamlyn asked.

Nathel shook his head. "Not necessarily. He can open portals to the Underworld, and he uses that to transport his prey. Takes a lot of effort out of him. Sometimes he eats them straight away, occasionally he plays with the bodies. The longest lived for a week or so." He stared at the floor. "There's no point in resisting him."

"We're going to go tonight and stop him," Tamlyn said. "Blow him to bits and get the hostages to safety."

"What about my family?"

"Your family will be safe," Tamlyn promised. "Your little brother will have a future."

"And when he returns?" Nathel demanded.

"He won't be back," Lukie said. "I guarantee you, this will be his final night."

Nathel chewed soundlessly for a few seconds. "Okay. All or nothing."

CHAPTER 19
REVENANT HUNTING
4:00AM, 8 BLOODSTONE 2003

THEY FOLLOWED Nathel through the wild and tangled garden of the Clearwater estate. Tamlyn was dressed in black with a bulky, military-grade air shotgun slung over his back, and a heavy machete at his side.

Lukie held a Cubermarket shopping bag containing the meter-long shield. *Cage better still be around to use this thing.* He also had her photo, and she didn't want the Baron to get his hands on that.

If the Clearwaters had bothered with the tourist trade, they would have turned a profit. People from the big city loved tours of the various country mansions, ruins, and rustic inns that dotted the eastern coast. But the Clearwater place was abandoned, a perfect lair for a hungry corpse. Iron palings surrounded the grounds, which were a private jungle. Nathel led them through a side gate, through the overgrown brush, and past derelict stables. Beyond, the mansion itself squatted. Formed of two wings, it hunched over a central courtyard. Glazed, blue roof tiles glinted under the evening starlight. Nathel ducked away from the main entrance and led them through the old servants' door at the back. He clicked on a small flashlight and guided them into the house.

Lukie had always been pissed at school when Nathel, who lived in an actual *mansion,* had never invited her or the band home. At least now she knew why.

The servants' corridors—all worn stone floors and plaster walls—snaked through the building, allowing the staff to work without being seen by the Clearwaters. The main house could be glimpsed—parlors and sitting rooms with the furniture shrouded in sheets, hallways lined with grim-faced portraits of the Clearwater lineage.

Nathel showed them to the ground library. His flashlight beam slid past leather-bound books ensconced in oaken shelves and a suit of armor standing upwards to attention, glaive in hand. He stopped in front of a bookcase and studied it carefully before pulling on a book on the third shelf.

There was a click, and the wall of books swiveled to one side, revealing a secret passage with stairs leading downward.

"You disappoint me, Nathel." A silhouette peeled away from shadows, and the Baron limped forth. In the real world, devoid of his shadowy cloak, the Baron was a flayed figure of gray tendons and dark, raw meat. "Betraying our family legacy."

Nathel didn't say anything. He drew the gun that Tamlyn had loaned him and pointed it at the Baron with trembling hands.

"Come now," Brandas commanded. "Both you and I know that I can't be defeated. Drop the weapon."

Nathel stood back. "Lukie?" His voice cracked.

"Want this?" Lukie ran forward, waving the wooden trophy shield at the Baron.

The Baron fell into a pool of shadow onto the floor. A second later, the darkness had reformed around her feet. Raw meat hands and arms stretched out, pulling Lukie down. She held the shield up in the air, holding it out of the Baron's reach.

The Baron rose out of the gloom with a bestial growl, snatching at her. "How dare you profane—

"Shoot!" Lukie screamed just as Tamlyn appeared from the corridor, pumping his shotgun at the Baron's back repeatedly.

She had heard all her life that the air weapons were supposed to be quiet, but the shotgun filled the room with its loud retorts. It hadn't been the best plan—*I'll distract him, you shoot him and don't worry about hitting me because I'm dead anyway*—but it worked. Pellet spray peppered the Baron. Black vapor oozed from his wounds.

Tamlyn fired the shotgun again, just as Nathel screamed incoherently and fired as well.

Shot peppered the leather-bound books and the gilded portraits.

Lukie held the Baron's struggling, smoke-ridden body in place as Tamlyn hacked off the revenant's head with the machete. Gray mist drifted up from his neck stump. A heartbeat later and the rest of his body vaporised.

"That was it?" Nathel said incoherently. "That wasn't even a minute."

Tamlyn removed his ear plugs. "I guess he wasn't used to being attacked by professionals."

Lukie dug at the pellets in her skin. Darkness oozed around the holes in her body, cleansing her wounds. Unlike Brandas, she was still intact.

"Yes," Tamlyn said. "Now let's get those kids out."

Lukie hefted up the shield and trotted down the secret passageway. Tamlyn made a face, covering his mouth and nose. Lukie inhaled, and a reek of blood and decomposing flesh flooded through her senses.

She'd been expecting a proper medieval dungeon with

iron maidens, racks, and cells, but this was a modern concrete box.

Cage was in one corner, and two bodies were chained to the wall. A male ogre: Gerron. Smashed and mangled.

The second figure was Maz. Lying on the cold floor, unchained, but with her eyes closed and breathing raggedly. Lukie dropped the shopping bag with the shield, transferred her artefacts to her jeans pockets, stripped off her jacket and draped it over the woman's still form.

Cage gave a weak gasp from the corner. He was a mess, his face slicked with feverish sweat, his legs broken and pointing the wrong way.

"I'm going upstairs to call an ambulance," Tamlyn said. "Get them loose." He raced up the stairs while Nathel shivered, rubbing his arms.

"Shit, you're hurt." Lukie crouched next to the hunter and, with a tug, snapped his chains from the wall.

"I heal fast," Cage rasped. "I'll be all right. In time."

"We shot the revenant, but he's going to come back."

"Yes," Cage said. "Unless I can perform a warding. But I'll need one of his artifacts—"

"Got it." She pressed the supermarket bag against his skin.

"And to know where he died—"

"The Pillars of Majesty," Lukie recalled. "That should free all the souls he has captured in Tenebra, correct?"

"No," Cage rasped, sitting up. "They'll all fall into the void."

"But that's not *fair*." Karra, Maz. The other people trapped in the endless party. They didn't deserve to become shades, or worse, prey.

"You could try to gain power over his realm in Tenebra by drinking his soul. If you can defeat him." Cage's expression was skeptical.

But she needed to do it. "I'll go in there and free every-one," Lukie said. "Get everybody out. You can ward the Pillars tomorrow."

"I'll give you permission to feed," Cage said.

"I need your permission?"

"A binding I did to you."

"We'll talk later." If she had time, she'd have serious words with him. But she didn't. "How do I get to Tenebra quickly?"

"I'll do it with this." Cage rested a blood-smeared arm against the shield.

"It will be over then?" Nathel interrupted in a small voice. "Before the next sunset?"

"Yes," Cage said. "One way or another. Ready, Lukie?"

She nodded and braced herself to fall once more into the sea of shadows.

CHAPTER 20
TENEBRA, AGAIN

THE FULL YELLOW moon shone down the night of the party. Ringlight arced overhead—a thin line of ice against the golden evening sky. The beach house she hated so much was there. Eternal. Perfectly preserved.

Music from 1963 played. The revelers' cars remained parked outside, never going anywhere.

Before, when she'd entered this world, she'd been the image of her living self.

But now, she needed to be an undead monster.

She didn't need to breathe or feel her heart race or smell the salt-laden wind sweeping in from the ocean. Instead, the blush faded from her skin and the ice-cold chill infused her. No blood flowed through her veins, only the smoke and substance of Tenebra. She thought of her eyes, red and glowing.

When she was fully formed, she ran up the stairs of the beach house.

The man with the horn-rimmed glasses opened the door for her, pointing a trembling hand forward and ducking back.

The party had stopped. Several people stood around in a

daze, while others, with more self-awareness, were pressed against the walls.

Brandas was in the center of the floor, holding down the woman with cat's eye spectacles. She changed to pale smoke in his hands—her discordant rhythm cut short.

The Baron was drinking souls.

The house of eternal guests wasn't just a place that Brandas had stocked with admirers.

It was also a larder.

Then he pushed past the dazed people near him—their souls previously chewed—and gripped Karra with one big hand.

"You promised—" she shrieked as the Baron pulled her close.

Karra had given him her loyalty in exchange for her survival, but the Baron couldn't even guarantee that. He was so entranced on his feeding that he wasn't paying attention as Lukie ran through the door, leaped up on the Baron's back, and wrapped her arms around his neck.

—bop-bop-bom-do-wap—

His soul music flattened her like a hammer. He let go of Karra, trying to throw Lukie off, but she tightly clutched him with her undead strength.

She replaced his droning baritone with the electric guitar crescendos of Invisible Youth, peeling away the substance of the Baron of Clearwater.

An old man showed Brandas around the crumbling estate. "Once we were peers of the realm. Companions of the king. Now, nothing. We lost everything in the People's Revolution. It was a lie; a true-blooded human can never be the equal of a sub-human elf or an inhuman ork. The Battle of Reladon was two thousand years ago, but it never ended."

Brandas roared, trying to tear Lukie from his back. His hands gripped the side of her neck, and he fed from her in retaliation as his baritone *bop-bop-bops* smothered her 80s rock. Memories were torn away, things she would never know again.

Lukie knifed him with a raging guitar solo, overwhelming his harmonies…

Reading books entitled Humanity and Supremacy ordered from Mr. Glover's news agency. Wanting to restore the Clearwater barony to the List of Peers, to claim the heritage their ancestors had so shamefully cast aside. It wasn't fair that the Clearwaters had gone from rulers of their country estate and crumbled into nobodies. He read the book under the covers at night, pondering how to be the Baron. For real.

Lukie was trying to absorb it all when Brandas tried a new tactic. Rather than feeding from her, ripping away her memories and soul-stuff, he dragged her to the moment of her death.

The sky was dark as she fled along the beach. Her heart pounded. Behind her, heavy footsteps pounded the sand.

Thick hands gripped her throat. She couldn't breathe. *That song! I'll never sing it with her—*

Her last living memory.

But that didn't worry her any more. She was an undead monster, and not prey. Her fingers closed on the cassette in her pocket and she thought of all the music she wanted to compose and play and would never get that chance. Her rage at her lost life crushed the Baron's harmonies under a thrashing beat, and she devoured the moment of his death.

———

The car wends its way along the cliff road, out of town. One side is a steep shelf of gray basalt, the other drops away to reveal an ocean. Brandas hits the accelerator, hand lazily gripping the wheel. He's been drinking. A six pack sits in the passenger seat next to him, an open can beside him in a plastic ring glued onto his dashboard. He's had two or three already, but he's Baron Shark, ruler of the local surfing club. It takes more than a few beers to slow him down.

He thinks about girls. About wanting to kill them. To squeeze them until they stop. His heart races: every part of him responds with eagerness.

I'll take a backpacker hitch-hiking up the coast road. Offer her a ride. Find a quiet place in the woods. If I pick a good location, they'll never discover her body. If it was the Middle Ages, I'd have my choice of all the peasant girls. It would be my sovereign right.

He's daydreaming, driving with one hand and stroking himself with the other. Not really watching the road. The bend he was expecting later looms up in his windshield. He slams the brakes. The car skids, slides, and crashes over the railing.

The Pillars of Majesty—the three wind-eroded limestone spears sticking out of the ocean—are the last thing he sees as the car smashes into them.

I never got to kill anyone.

An age of spinning darkness. A vision of a fortress within Tenebra; spindly towers rising in the air like skeletal fingers echoing the Baron's final view of the Pillars. Corpse-filled gibbets swing from the walls. A thin, cadaverous man walks atop the battlements, his face masked with blood.

Red Jack.

At first Lukie thought that she was still in Brandas's memories, but Jack saw her directly with gimlet eyes. "I'll *devour* you, servant of the Murder God. I'll destroy you, make you suffer like you wouldn't believe—"

CHAPTER 21
CRIMSON SUNRISE

CONTACT WITH BRANDAS'S disgusting patron was cut off like a dead telephone line when Lukie devoured the last spark of her murderer's soul. He vanished, but his essence hung within her, a slowly digesting Winterdark meal, and Lukie's mind was full of his droning baritone rhythm.

—bop-bop-bop—

Cage had said if she ate the Baron, she would control his house. But it wasn't like taking keys from a corpse. She needed to concentrate, assert her own music on top of the Baron's, but everything was sliding away. If she didn't get a grip on the Baron's soul fragments, she would throw them up like a meal of rotten fruit, and everyone would fall into the void.

—ma-ma-ra-ma-ma-ma-ra—

"Karra, I can't hold on to this place!" Lukie reached out a hand, but Karra pulled back, her eyes wide. Lukie's heart wrenched. Had she just saved Karra from being devoured by the Baron only to see her consumed by shades?

"What do you need?" Maz called out, pushing aside the blank-eyed, soul-chewed partygoers as she stepped forward.

"His music," Lukie wiped her lips. "It's too 1960s. I can't connect to it."

She thought of Vizzie Slanter. Green eyeshadow, slicked-back blonde hair, and powerful guitar. "Can you sing Invisible Youth? Twelve Corners?"

Maz frowned.

"I need 80s rock!" Lukie begged. "Otherwise I'm going to lose control."

"I don't know any 80s songs!" Maz said. "But what about some Brown Sugar Pop? They're 90s!" She warbled in a tuneless voice:

> "Gotta eat your pancakes, girls
> Gotta eat them right
> Maple syrup drops like pearls
> Ice cream, take a bite...."

Lukie tried to focus on the song, but nothing resonated. Her own internal music was now a whisper, ground down by the weight of the Baron's baritone drone.

A partygoer screamed as a crack appeared in front of the bandstand. The whispering of the Tenebran void filled the air.

—wap-wap-de-wap-bop-bop-bop—

"Does anyone know any 80s hits?" Maz called out. "Oh shit, what does Mom listen to again?"

Clawed, distended fingers reached out from the hole. People retreated to the corners of the room.

"You should have let him eat you!" A blonde girl in a beehive hairdo pointed at Karra. "At least he kept us safe."

A shade appeared near the drink table, claws outstretched.

Karra wiped her face, placed her hands by her side, and then sang in a clear soprano voice:

> "It's been a while since you went away,

I've stopped counting the passing days
Our last date remains my prize
When we watched the crimson sunrise…"

Lukie *knew* that song. It was *her* music. Crimson Sunrise. Memories blurred through her mind. Sitting in Whispers Café writing the lyrics with Karra. Rehearsing in her bedroom. Imagining what it would be like to sing it with Karra at the final end-of-school party. She got to her feet. Now she could focus on other things than the Baron's venomous earworm within her. With her control of his soul fragments, she sealed up the cracks in the house, forcing the shades back into the void.

"The stars all faded from the sky
The ring burned cold, the moon shut her eye
We put aside all our grief and lies
When we watched the crimson sunrise…"

Lukie joined in with Karra, singing the third verse in her rasping, undead voice:

"The waves rolled in on the morning tide
The wind swept across the pale cliff side
I looked into your beautiful eyes
And held your hand under the crimson
    sunrise…"

Everything fit in place now, became more stable and under her control. The people's outfits changed into the fashions of 1983—studded denim, spiked or teased hair, puffy jackets. In her mind's eye, she saw the big cars outside with their fins and hoods shift into the familiar, squarish models of the 1980s.

And her red Sunjoy waiting for her.

"What do you want us to do?" The man with the horn-rimmed glasses adjusted his new leather jacket. "Keep on dancing?"

The silence in the room was palpable.

Karra folded her arms. Maz twisted her hands together in supplication.

No one wanted to be stuck again in another forever-party. Even if the music and fashions would be a thousand times better.

"No," Lukie said. "This party's over." She needed a way to get everybody home, or at least, out of the dismal realm of Tenebra. She ached for her old room, for years of school and the hope she had for the party. She thought of her cassette, with its promise of study at the Conservatorium of Music and pulled out her car keys, used for a vehicle intended for a journey she'd never gotten the chance to take.

The Lanes of the Dead are open for you. It was her patron's voice, but no longer sounding like an angry child.

She *knew* then how to guide the souls on. Not with a burst of power within her, but with a slowly unfolding revelation.

"Everyone!" Lukie jingled her keys. "Get into your cars and give as many people a lift as you can. No one gets left behind."

———

Lukie walked with Karra down the driveway to where the Sunjoy waited.

"That song. I came back to sing it to you. But it didn't feel like a love song when we performed."

"It's not a love song." Karra glanced at the darkening sky. "It's a break-up song."

"We were breaking up?" Lukie stopped. "I know I lost

memories—I've been in the void for a long time and the Baron chewed on me—but I forgot that?"

"Yeah. Things weren't the same anymore. We were both moving to Storm City, but in different directions. You were going to the Con, and I was off to the University of Technology to study biology. We agreed it was best to have a friendly breakup."

Lukie tightened her hands, trying to imagine a world where they would both be alive and forty-ish, like Tamlyn. Would Lukie have been the world's greatest musician or just someone performing in pubs on the weekend? Would Karra have become a great scientist?

They'd never know that now. Those lives were lost forever. All she could do was move on. She got in her car and gripped the steering wheel.

Maz slid into the back seat, and Karra rode in front. Outside, all the partygoers were squeezing into their own vehicles. Some of the soul-chewed people were pushed into seats by others. No one was left behind.

She started the engine. Crimson Sunrise played within her mind, guiding her forward.

She drove down the Beach House's driveway, signalled, and turned left on the road to Storm City, past the Pillars of Majesty where Brandas had died.

Behind them, the other cars followed, their headlights cutting through the gloom of Tenebra.

A white mist rolled in, covering the world outside the windscreen.

"Stop here!" Karra shouted.

Lukie braked hard.

Karra opened the passenger door, revealing a green hillside.

A thin road wended its way ahead. In the distance, the voices, laughter, and tinny music of a country fair echoed.

Karra's face lit up with wonder. She looked so happy and gentle that Lukie felt stunned. She'd never really seen this expression before. No, it was as though Lukie had never known the real Karra after all, had only dated and danced with her masks and shadows.

The new Karra kissed Lukie. A farewell kiss. And one of forgiveness. A silver tear gleamed on her cheek. Then she undid her seatbelt, got out, and walked away from the car.

Lukie almost followed. She tightened her hand on the steering wheel. But she had to drive Maz home safely, wherever that was. And guide the others on their way.

"Lukie?" Maz asked, poking her.

"Yeah, yeah." Lukie wiped her face and drove onwards down a long, dark highway.

CHAPTER 22
AFTER

5:01AM, 8 BLOODSTONE 2003

LUKIE WOKE up on the beach, cold water lapping at her legs. She rose to her feet, not bothering to brush the sand from her clothing or empty her boots.

The sun was rising above the ocean, touching the sky with gold and orange.

Lukie wasn't scared of death. She raised eternally chill, pallid hands to the coming light, awaiting its final touch.

She'd had a second chance, which was more than most victims did. She'd killed the Baron—*eaten his very soul*—and stopped his thirty-year murder spree around Breakwater Bay. Karra and the people that had been trapped in Tenebra were somewhere else. Lukie wasn't sure where they all were exactly—the Lanes of the Dead were labyrinthine and confusing—but the places she'd guided them to were better than the Underworld.

Her final night was over.

I wish I could have spoken with Dad one more time. And composed more songs like Crimson Sunrise. So many things I never got the chance to do. I wonder if anyone dies fully satisfied with their life?

The sun crested the horizon, a giant ball of liquid light that covered the ocean with golden roads.

Lukie closed her eyes as the rays touched. She didn't want to watch herself dissolve into smoke.

A dull lassitude crept through her limbs.

She waited to unravel back into shadow.

But nothing happened. Lukie opened her eyes. The sun was up now. It was dawn, and she still existed—weak, cold, and not-breathing. She clenched her hands, but her super-strength was gone. And her sense of Tenebra had withered inside of her. Not forever, but it was distant under the sun's radiant light.

Over the past night, she'd gathered her memories. There were some that weren't hers: a sky clouded by smog, worn brick buildings jammed together, 1940s-style cars rumbling along narrow highways.

"Why do I still have your vestige?" Lukie asked, focusing on those other images and the other within.

You can borrow it for a bit longer, her patron's voice rasped in her head.

"But why? You said I hurt you. I'm so over doing that."

To tell the truth, I wasn't doing a lot before you came along. Just sitting around, brooding, until you scratched on my door like a stray cat. It was like cutting off my arm to help you, but I also felt pain because part of me was waking up again. You reminded me of being in the world again, working on a case.

"Now what?"

I'm going to reopen my detective agency. Interested?

"Aren't you just a little kid?"

I'm seventeen.

"But that's not old enough to run an agency."

Rubbish. I solved the mystery of the abandoned lighthouse, the haunting of Tegram Manor, and the locked room disappearance of

Harlowe Coppermine. Cases that the regular cops couldn't even crack.

"Red Jack called you the Murder God."

It's just a spooky title. I prefer the 'Dark Detective.' Many of the ghost lords are killers. Butchers like Red Jack, poisoners like the Lady of One Thousand Whispers or madwomen like the Blood Queen. They send their revenants back to the world to hunt and feed. We can work to stop them. And free all the souls they trap.

"Deal," Lukie said. Red Jack *had* threatened her. There would be a reckoning later.

A connection, heavy and tangible, sparked between her and the Dark Detective.

I'll be in touch about the next case. The direct sense of her patron's consciousness retreated, leaving Lukie alone on the beach.

Lukie stretched. Now she had more time. She had to work out what to do with it, to try to survive as a soul-eating monster. But at least she could choose what kind of monster she was going to be.

———

"That's what happened," Lukie told Tamlyn as he drove into the hospital parking lot.

"You should get a hearse if you're driving dead people to their afterlife," Tamlyn mused, finishing his bagel. He yawned and rubbed at his bloodshot eyes. "Not some old Sunjoy."

"It's *my* car," she said, wishing it was here now rather than in Tenebra.

"You're feeling okay?"

Lukie shrugged. "I'm as weak as a kitten. No super-strength. I can't hear people's soul music. No wonder the Baron hid during the day."

"Did you want me to come in with you?"

"I'll be fine. I'll call you on the walkie talkie…"

"Cell phone."

"On the phone if I get into trouble." She held up the small device, marveling at it. She really was in the future.

———

Cage was in his hospital bed watching early morning cartoons, his silver hair spread over the sky-blue pillows. His legs were covered in plaster.

"He's gone," Lukie said.

"Good." Cage kept watching the television set. "I'll still need to ward the Pillars before sundown."

Lukie shrugged. She knew the Baron was dealt with, but it didn't hurt to be thorough. "I'll let Tam know." She wasn't sure how they were going to get Cage released from the hospital in his current state, but they'd figure something out.

Silence dragged.

"I'd like my photo back, please." Lukie folded her arms. "And for you to take that ward off me so I can feed without asking permission. I'm in control now."

"No."

"No?" Lukie hadn't expected that. "But I helped you defeat the Baron. I'm not a ravenous predator like him."

Cage shook his head.

"What is your problem?" Lukie fumed, tempted to poke at his plaster-covered legs.

"I have to protect the world from monsters," Cage said. "Even tame ones."

"How many times do I have to prove myself to you?"

"All the time," Cage said.

Fuming, she left. Before she broke another bone in his body.

———

She went by Maz's room on her way out of the hospital but didn't go in. The woman was awake and blinking, surrounded by people. "I had the strangest dream," she was saying. "A party that never ended. And everyone kept changing costume. Where's my man?"

Not sure of what to say, Lukie walked away. Gerron hadn't been at the party, so she hadn't guided his soul. He'd probably been eaten by the Baron. But there was also a chance he was lost within Tenebra. *I'll see if I can find him out there tonight when my powers return…*

———

Lukie walked up to the front desk where a nurse was clacking away at a typewriter connected to a television screen. "Excuse me, how is Nathel Clearwater doing?"

"Still in surgery," the nurse said after tapping on her keyboard. She opened her mouth to say something and then closed it again. *She doesn't think he'll make it.* "Did you want me to leave your number for when you can see him?"

Lukie read off the string of digits she'd written on the back of her hand.

"I'm checking myself out." A rough-voiced man walked up to the desk.

Relief swabbed through Lukie. Terek was still alive and sane. She wasn't sure how to feel about him now. He'd hurt Karra all those years ago, but he had also been one of Nathel's victims. And she'd damaged his soul with her first feeding. She would let him go. "Terek! How are you feeling?"

"Fine." Terek grunted. "Do I know you?"

"I visited your bar. It was a great place."

Terek gave a sleazy smile. "You should stop by tonight. I'll give you a free drink."

"Um, I heard there was a fight there last night."

"What?" Terek rolled up his sleeves. "Who did it?"

"Some tourists. I'll be sure to visit next time I'm in town," Lukie promised just as Terek stalked past her, grumbling, ignoring the demands of the nurse behind him.

———

Tamlyn was listening to country music as he waited in his car. Lukie slid into the passenger seat.

"Cage won't lift that curse." Lukie punched the dashboard. Her cold fist thumped the faux-wood paneling. "I don't know what to do."

"We'll sort something out," Tamlyn promised. "I'm picking him up this evening so he can do his thing at the Pillars. I'll have a private chat with him. He might listen to me."

"He better. I'm not following Cage around like a stray cat. I've got to find Dad."

"He's at Storm City," Tamlyn said. "I have his address. Police magic."

"Oh wow!" Lukie sat up. Now she had to work out how to explain herself to him. *But he's Dad. Everything will be fine.*

Or would it? "What if Nathel dies? Why did he shoot himself? We defeated Brandas. He was free."

Tamlyn sighed. "I found a note when I went back to investigate the library. He knew there'd be questions about the basement. He wanted us to blame it all on him. Help his family."

"But he didn't need to!" Lukie chewed at her knuckles. "We could have worked something out."

"You can't predict how people will react to this sort of

thing, Everyone's got scars. You just have to be strong enough to carry them."

Lukie briefly wished for a do-over of that final night in 1983. Save Karra. Stop the Baron. Help the band be friends again. Assist Nathel to run away. She rubbed at her eyes, missing the sensation of being able to cry.

It had taken her death to understand how much damage she'd done. And now she needed to learn from it, to use her powers to seek out other monsters and rescue their victims.

"I got you a present." Tamlyn handed her a box.

It was a bulky CD set: 'The Greatest Hits of the Eighties and Nineties.'

"All right!" Lukie held it up, feeling better. "Let's see what I missed!"

———

Find out what happens when Lukie goes home to meet her father, twenty years after her death, in Feral Night, the second book of the Revenant Records.

AUTHOR'S NOTE

Thanks for reading this—my first published book.

Listen, I've got a confession to make. While I've always dreamed of being a writer, I've never been good at finishing my creative works. I have over nine trunked novels, many intended to be the start of an epic fantasy series. I conceived and wrote most of them during that phase in life when you think you'll live forever, and that you've got all the time in the world to finish your books, and be the next famous author talked about on forums and in bookshops.

Then the COVID years hit. I spent months locked up in my study, hearing reports of death and gloom everywhere, and facing the fact that I wouldn't live forever, and might never publish anything.

And even I wrote a book, would my craft allow to communicate all the ideas for my characters, world and stories to my readers?

I knew I could finish big writing projects, having written and developed them for the dayjob. Why couldn't I do the same for my fantasy books? What was holding me back?

Anxiety. During COVID, I had time to work through a

bunch of personal baggage, and one of those was a fear that my creative works would never be good enough. (I remember being like that as a kid—I made a clay castle for a school presentation in pottery class and destroyed it as I thought it was terrible, even though I was eight, and adults are incredibly enthused by kid's creations when you're that age.) One of my COVID realizations was that you don't get good by not writing; you get good by writing more. A lot of my favorite books and television shows 'got good' after the initial episodes or season. I wasn't sure how long it would take me to achieve the standard I wanted, but now was the time to start. My goal for this series is to make each book better than the next last. Push the lead characters, and their friendship, into different directions. Dig more into the world and backstory, after getting people interested in this first one.

Final Night was born out of fears of death. And desire to play with undead tropes. Originally Lukie was a vampire, but after I introduced the soul-eating stuff, and that you had to make a pact to come back as an undead, initial beta readers warned I was wandering too far away what made the creatures recognizable at 'vampires', so the revenants shambled free from Tenebra. Other themes that emerged during the writing (and re-writing) were about change, change, culture shock, redemption and descending to the Underworld to rescue someone, only to find they weren't deliriously happy you showed up. It's a good story, but I'm also pumped about what's coming next, and how the characters develop. Stay around and I'll show you. (I've got a newsletter at http://kell shaw.com/newsletter that would be the best way to stay in contact with me and my plans.)

If you enjoyed this book, help other readers like you discover it by leaving a review. This really helps grow the readership, and keeps me incentivized to keep writing these stories. Thank you.

Now, read on for a look at the sequel, Feral Night, to see what happens when Lukie goes home to reconnect with her father.

FERAL NIGHT
BOOK TWO OF THE REVENANT RECORDS

Return to Kell Shaw's Vestiges of Magic world in a knife-edge sequel.

Lukie's father is trapped in the Underworld and it's all her fault.

Twenty years after her murder, Lukie has returned to life and is ready to go home, but her father isn't willing to believe his beloved daughter is back from the dead. Before she can reconcile with him, a supernatural predator steals her father's soul. One that she's led straight to his door, after foolishly ignoring the signs that something was amiss.

To get her father back, Lukie must uncover the true nature of the ancient horror haunting Thunderhead Ward before a spectral hunt of bestial ghosts is unleashed upon the world.

And she only has until midnight on New Year's Eve, when the borders between the dead and living lands seal, or her father will be lost forever…

FERAL NIGHT: CHAPTER ONE

LUKENARIA CARPENTER HURRIED through the dark, suburban streets of the Thunderhead Ward toward her father's house, working out what to say to him after being dead for twenty years:

Hey Dad! I'm back! I'm a walking corpse, but it's okay. We'll work something out.

No. Too sudden.

Hey, Dad! It's me! You know how everyone says the Age of Magic ended, or never existed? Well, bits of it are still around, and if you make a pact with a powerful entity, you can get their vestige and—

No. Keep it simple.

Dad, I missed you! I have so much to tell you—

That was it!

We'll spend all night talking and it will be amazing.

Both sides of the street were lined with red brick houses, immaculate driveways and neatly clipped lawns. With her undead vision, Lukie easily discerned the number on the nearest letter box. Number 7. Getting close. She had to hurry. Tamlyn Tanner might wake any second, realize that she'd flipped through his notebook when he hadn't been looking, and cut short her reunion with Dad. Once he'd been her friend in high school and they'd been the same age. Now he was nearly forty, and a police inspector, while she still looked seventeen.

"Stay away from your father," Tamlyn had told Lukie. "Give him space and——"

"No!" Lukie had shouted. "That's not how we do things! We trust each other like that!" and she'd crooked her fingers together.

She missed her father terribly. For most of Lukie's existence, he had been her sole parent: always there for her, grounding her flights of fancy with rock-solid certainty, fielding all her questions about life, school and relationships.

Twenty years ago, she'd gone to a party and been murdered. It had taken her that long to escape the Underworld, making a pact with her ghost lord patron to become a revenant and return to the world in her physical form. While her memories were fragmented, she remembered saying goodbye to Dad before she died. Getting her new car from him as a gift, kissing him farewell and promising to be home before midnight. And she'd never returned.

Now she was back, and once she explained everything, she and her father would resume their relationship as though she'd never been gone. Soon, she would be *there* and he'd give her a warm hug, and—

Bestial howls echoed. She stopped, whirled around, trying to determine where the sound of wolves was coming from.

The empty streets mocked her.

A piece of paper skittered along the street on the night wind. Parked cars sat in their carports and driveways, their sleek, modern 2003 shapes another sign that Lukie was no longer in 1983. She remembered to breathe and the smell of the area flooded her nostrils: pollen from flowering bushes, fresh-turned dirt, and the reek of chlorine from nearby pools.

And yet no sign of any dogs, apart from a faint yip-yip-yip sound from a distant terrier.

Perhaps she'd overheard a movie. No, then the sound would have come from a direction she could have pinpointed.

She paused and studied the empty streets, and then the howls echoed again, within the space of her own mind.

Something supernatural had to be going on. She thrust her senses outward, reaching for Tenebra and the realm of the dead. The Veil, a metaphysical barrier, separated from the living lands from Tenebra. Most times when Lukie perceived it, it had the solidity of a psychic cinderblock wall. Right now, it felt as flimsy as a shower curtain. The sense of the Underworld pushed against Lukie like a dark, lapping tide, and beyond that, a presence loom.

Someone was watching her from the other side.

"Hello?" Lukie tried. The observer pulled back, distant. Without rending through the Veil into Tenebra itself, Lukie did not know who or what it was.

She decided against crossing over. Tenebra was no place for a casual visit. Rather than the nice, gray purgatorial land of the dead that popped up in folklore and religion stories, Tenebra was horrible. It was a void, a tar pit full of trapped souls that consumed each other to survive. Some ran, some hunted, while others learned to build pocket dimensions in the darkness from their memories and obsessions, the most powerful becoming the ghost lord sovereigns of the Underworld. Lukie reached for her vestige—her patron's soul fragment within her—but her own ghost lord's presence was distant. No straightforward answers there.

She bit her lip. She didn't have time for distractions, she

needed to see Dad before she exploded within, before Tamlyn came.

Weird stuff from Tenebra could wait.

Dismissing the howls and looming presence from her mind, Lukie checked a nearby castle-shaped letterbox: 23. Nearly there. She made sure that the sunglasses were still on —concealing her undead eyes—and sprinted until she arrived at her father's home: 47 Barbican Street. The two story, red brick house, with its manicured hedges, rose gardens, and the wide-spreading oak tree in the front yard was straight from a television show.

Why did Dad move here? It's nowhere near the beach.

The Thunderhead Ward was ten hours' drive from Break-water Bay, up the coast and inland. Tamlyn had contacted her father in person to tell him the official story about how she'd been killed and why. Giving some resolution. And yet, when Tamlyn returned to their motel, he'd refused to disclose any juicy details, apart from that her father was fine. As usual, Tamlyn had said they'd 'talk later' and they never did. No, that was not—

Another howl.

What is going on? She hesitated. Was she putting Dad in danger? Cage had warned her that the mortal world of sunlight, pizza and school was no longer her province. Barriers sealed it away from the hidden shores of the super-natural realm, and those should not be breached.

No. Lukie curled her hands into fists. She had to speak to her father.

But how?

Did she knock and announce herself? Whisper to him through a wall?

She approached the front door, listening to the night breeze.

A faint, familiar snore rattled the air.

She knew that snore! Right in the downstairs living room! She squinted through a gap in the curtains.

A figure sprawled on a brown couch, a rough blanket pulled over him. Who was that elderly man? Why did he sound like Dad? He turned in his sleep, revealing his profile.

Her father, but different. Bald, with a lined face and a visible paunch. No longer the muscular father from her memory.

Maybe this isn't such a good idea, Lukie considered. *Perhaps I should wait for Tam —*

Dad snored, grunted and woke. He sat bolt upright, rubbing his head as though emerging from a terrible dream.

And he stared straight at her through the window.

"Hey Dad," Lukie rasped. "I'm back."

"Lukie?" Dad's face paled with shock. His hands shook and fumbled by his side. He walked slowly to the glass pane between them. "No. It can't be. You're dead."

She swallowed. Dad wasn't supposed to be like this: old, trembling and worst of all, doubting her existence. She forced her husky, undead voice into its former register. "I... returned from the Underworld. To see you." Not the greatest of introductions, but once they talked, everything would be fine. When she'd broken her bike or faked an assignment or lost track of time and broken curfew, all she needed to do was to speak to him. "I'm real, Dad!"

He retreated a step. "I saw your body on the slab. And what he did to you..."

"I got the Baron, Dad," Lukie explained. "The guy that killed me and Karra. Sucked his soul dry."

Rather than being reassured, Dad's eyes widened in shock.

Crap. Now was not the best time to explain to her father she was a horrible, undead monster. She raised her hands in the air. "Look, I'm doing this all wrong. Can we start again?

Please. I've come back from the dead. I'm a revenant. Like a zombie, but more awesome. I'm still me, and—"

"You *can't* be her. Lukie was cremated. We sprinkled her ashes on the beach—"

"You don't need your body to be a revenant," Lukie's frustration mounted. Why didn't he believe her? She was *right in front of him*. Her head throbbed and spectral energy bloomed around her. The weird presence from earlier was closer. No, this was more important. "I was trapped in the Underworld for twenty years, but then I got out and—"

"My daughter is safe in the afterlife with her mother. I don't know what you are—demon, hallucination—leave me alone!" He slid the blinds shut. Muffled sobs echoed.

"Dad, please no. Don't cry, it's really me!" She thumped on the door, intending to knock, but the wood splintered off its hinges at her undead might. "Sorry!"

She peered into the gap. Inside was a modern living room: couch, bookshelves, a carpeted floor and large television. Impossibly neat and lacking the familiar clutter of guitars, surfboards and car magazines that resembled the old house she'd shared with Dad twenty years ago. Her father huddled on the carpet, frozen.

Lukie gritted her teeth. One more try. "Sorry about the door. I'll fix it. Please, give me a chance to explain."

The sense of the presence from earlier rose again, like a mantle. *Piss off*, Lukie thought. *I don't have time for you.*

She turned her attention to her father, trying to figure out the best way to get him to see *her* and not some undead horror, when a girl in blue pajamas rushed in front of her. Perhaps thirteen, with long dark hair and the tan coloring of the Varuvals, the Stormfield's traditional peasantry. Also: completely human and not half elven like Lukie.

The girl brandished a piece of antler. "You don't belong here. Begone!"

"Who are you?" Lukie stopped in her tracks.

"His real daughter," the girl challenged. "A wizard of great power!" She stabbed the horn wand directly in the air.

"What are you talking about?" Lukie growled. A wizard? *Really?* Normal mortals weren't supposed to know about the supernatural realm. Cage had said that ancient rituals protected the ordinary world from what remained of the magical. Yet that paled against the fact that she'd been *replaced*. Dad had remarried and gotten a proper human daughter. In Lukie's fragmented memories, she'd only kissed her father goodbye a few weeks ago; and now she'd been forgotten; substituted with a newer, better model.

She grated, "Go. Away," and stretched a hand to shove the girl aside.

The 'wizard' struck Lukie's arm with the antler, which shattered into a dozen horn shards. A sharp pain stabbed through Lukie's entire undead form and her limbs became molasses. She staggered, arms flailing, and her sunglasses slipped off, revealing her blank, red glowing eyes. She grunted, stunned. What was going on?

The mounting layers of spectral energy erupted.

A howl echoed and a hunched, canine-like humanoid figure bounded through the broken door and lunged at the girl.

Lukie struggled to her feet. Damn it; she'd heard those howls earlier and dismissed them. She'd led the creature *here* where it could prey on her father. Her impatience had put everyone in danger. And now she couldn't fix her mess and save the New Girl, as annoying as she was.

Sluggishness gripped her limbs—that antler, whatever it was—prevented her from dealing with the monster immediately.

"Sienna!" Dad shouted and charged at the creature, distracting it from clawing the girl.

The dog-thing stood on its hind legs and knocked Lukie's father to the carpet with a single swipe of its clawed fingers.

The hiss of spectral energy rippled in Lukie's ears. Undead fed off souls. And this thing was draining Dad, even as she'd drained the Baron's existence.

No, no! She'd only wanted to talk! To catch-up! She tried to shout, but no sound escaped her lips. Instead, she screamed inside, wishing for a chance to do this again, correctly from the beginning.

Sienna fumbled on the floor for her broken antler.

Finally, the lassitude left Lukie's limbs. She rushed at the creature, tackling it. She sensed souls as aural phenomena, and the monster seethed with chaotic music: chiming gongs and wailing screams. And overriding that was a simple, acoustic guitar melody, like the ones her father had played to her on Bellsday evening after they came home from the Surf Club.

Lukie staggered with horror. That was *Dad's soul*. Not drained, but collected.

The creature had stolen her father.

And it was all her fault.

"Give him back!" she yelled as she attempted to strangle the creature.

The dog-thing reared, and threw her against a nearby bookcase, which cracked and broke.

Dad slumped on the floor, not moving while the girl screamed and clung to him.

The dog-thing lunged away through the front garden, reaching the dark street and sprinting into the night.

"I'm sorry!" Lukie cried. "I'll fix everything! I'll get him back, I promise!"

A light clicked on upstairs. Footsteps echoed.

This new family could deal with Dad's fallen form; she would track that monster and save his soul.

She turned and gave chase, stifling a scream, her hands curling into fists.

She'd ruined the lives of the people she cared about.

Again.

————

Interested? Visit https://kellshaw.com/feral-night to get your copy today.

BONUS MATERIAL

Enjoyed Final Night? Ready to see a short story that takes place between book 1 and 2?

I've written a special short story that takes place between this book and the next one. You can grab it from here: https://kellshaw.com/bonus

While you're there, sign up for my newsletter to be the first hear about new releases, bonuses and more at https://kellshaw.com/newsletter

ACKNOWLEDGMENTS

Firstly, this story and other works in this setting were developed during the Bestseller Academy online writing course, which kept me focused on my writing dreams during the pandemic madness. A big thanks to the two Marks, for making that possible.

I'd also like to thank my alpha readers and writing group peeps from that course: Academates/alumni—Lynne Clark, Mark Hood, Adam Jarvis, Tara Marakat, Rose Thompson, Chris Willis, Wendy, and Mary.

A big thanks to my other writing group, SIRIUS, which read earlier versions of the story—Georgina Ballantine, Patricia Bernard, Ferne Merrylees, Kwame Slusher and JZ Ting.

And other friends who answered the call to adventure and gave their thoughts on previous drafts—Matt Cramp, Malcolm Edwards, Jay, Stephen Neal and Adam Windsor.

Special thanks to Angela Slatter, for brutal developmental editing, Nef House Publishing for copyediting and proofreading, and Michael Christie and Charlotte Brogden for last-round proofing.

ALSO BY KELL SHAW IN THE VESTIGES OF MAGIC UNIVERSE

The Cambion Chronicles

1. Reflections Upon the Anniversary of My Descent

2. The Demon's Peace (forthcoming)

The Revenant Records

1. Final Night

2. Feral Night

3. Fractured Night

And various other tales as listed on: https://kellshaw.com/shorts

ABOUT THE AUTHOR

Kell Shaw is an author and avid tabletop roleplaying gamer, whose lifelong passion for fantasy—especially Shadowrun, the Lord of the Rings, and the World of Darkness—inspired him to create the Vestiges of Magic urban fantasy universe. Kell's fascination lies with the modern world colliding with magic, and his stories explore the lives of individuals caught between these realms.

Identifying as queer, Kell is committed to writing diverse characters who embark on thrilling adventures, and who aren't defined by their love lives. He released the first book of the Revenant Records saga in 2022, following an undead teenage detective who wants to grow up despite being forever seventeen.

Based in Sydney, Australia with his partner and beloved feline companions, Kell's diverse career has included roles as a technical writer, risk analyst, and project manager.

Sign up for Kell's newsletter at https://kellshaw.com/newsletter to receive free short stories and stay up-to-date with his latest projects.

facebook.com/KellShawAuthor

goodreads.com/kellshaw

dice.camp/@kellshaw

bsky.app/profile/kellshaw.com

instagram.com/KellShawAuthor